Tally slid back into a hard, planed chest, turning in his arms.

Her breath hitched, and she could see he'd heard. His pupils widened an instant before his eyes narrowed. His arm banded around her, drawing her closer, and she couldn't find the words or will to stop this. It was just a kiss.

Just...one...kiss... Then so much more.

His mouth skimmed over hers, once, twice, sending a pulse of desire through her. The mere touch of his lips to hers had her melting against him, her hands twisting in the fabric of his shirt. He slid his wrist from the sling and wrapped both arms around her, pressing to the small of her back.

She looped her arms around his neck. It had been so long since she'd been with a man. But even that didn't explain the depth of her longing to be with this man.

Marshall was so strong and thoughtful. But also mysterious in a way that intrigued her. Too much.

What was she thinking to kiss him this way? To lose sight of everything she'd come here to accomplish? Regret stinging, she eased back, struggling for words to explain why this shouldn't have happened. Of course, she couldn't share those reasons, none of which should be spoken. The secrets she hid would only hurt him.

So she simply held up her hands and backed away from the greatest temptation of her life.

* * *

The Rancher's Seduction is part of the Alaskan Oil Barons series from *USA TODAY* bestselling author Catherine Mann!

Dear Reader,

As a reader myself, I love Christmas stories, especially ones with large sweeping casts of characters gathering for the holidays. That made writing *The Rancher's Seduction* all the more fun since the Steeles and Mikkelsons are celebrating their first blended-family Christmas. Holidays are also times of heightened emotions, and that's no exception for Marshall Steele and Tally Benson!

Even though it wasn't Christmastime when I wrote this story, I enjoyed setting the mood with evergreen candles, carols and a fire in the fireplace. I savored more than a little hot chocolate and gingerbread! It's definitely fun celebrating the Christmas spirit anytime of the year.

Wishing you and yours a wonderful holiday season!

Cheers,

Catherine Mann

www.CatherineMann.com

CATHERINE MANN

THE RANCHER'S SEDUCTION

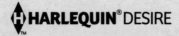

Recycling programs
for this product may
not exist in your area.

ISBN-13: 978-1-335-97191-3

The Rancher's Seduction

Copyright © 2018 by Catherine Mann

All rights reserved. Except for use in any review, the reproduction or
utilization of this work in whole or in part in any form by any electronic,
mechanical or other means, now known or hereafter invented, including
xerography, photocopying and recording, or in any information storage
or retrieval system, is forbidden without the written permission of the
publisher, Harlequin Enterprises Limited, 22 Adelaide St. West, 40th Floor,
Toronto, ON M5H 4E3, Canada.

This is a work of fiction. Names, characters, places and incidents are
either the product of the author's imagination or are used fictitiously,
and any resemblance to actual persons, living or dead, business
establishments, events or locales is entirely coincidental.

This edition published by arrangement with Harlequin Books S.A.

For questions and comments about the quality of this book,
please contact us at CustomerService@Harlequin.com.

® and TM are trademarks of Harlequin Enterprises Limited or its
corporate affiliates. Trademarks indicated with ® are registered in the
United States Patent and Trademark Office, the Canadian Intellectual
Property Office and in other countries.

Printed in U.S.A.

www.Harlequin.com

USA TODAY bestselling author **Catherine Mann** has won numerous awards for her novels, including both a prestigious RITA® Award and an *RT Book Reviews* Reviewers' Choice Award. After years of moving around the country bringing up four children, Catherine has settled in her home state of South Carolina, where she's active in animal rescue. For more information, visit her website, catherinemann.com.

Books by Catherine Mann

Harlequin Desire

Alaskan Oil Barons

The Baby Claim
The Double Deal
The Love Child
The Twin Birthright
The Second Chance
The Rancher's Seduction

Visit her Author Profile page at Harlequin.com, or catherinemann.com, for more titles.

To Vickie Gerlach—
a dear reader and treasured friend!

One

Tallulah Benson had been told at a young age that she'd been given an exciting name to go with a fairy-tale future. She just wished her life hadn't stalled out at the floor-sweeping version of Cinderella. No crystal slippers for her. She spent her days in sneakers.

She climbed the icy steps to the porch on the sprawling ranch home. To call it a log cabin would be an understatement since the two-story structure sported over eight thousand square feet—or so the job assignment had stated.

Bottom line, Tallulah—Tally—was grateful to have steady work as a housekeeper to pay her bills. If this latest gig cleaning for one of the oil-wealthy Steele family members went well, her résumé would be padded for more jobs cleaning for the rich and famous, which carried a substantial bump in her hourly rate. She needed the work. Both of her parents had died before her eighteenth birthday. She had no cushy savings or family safety net to fall back on.

By nineteen, she'd learned all too well how harsh life could be when no one had her back. Ten years hadn't dimmed the pain of giving up her baby for adoption, even knowing she'd made the right decision for her newborn son. These days, she controlled her life.

Tally stabbed the doorbell, the tones pealing through the walls of rancher Marshall Steele's home.

Marshall had used a twice-a-week cleaning service in the past. But a recent accident during a rodeo had left him with a broken arm during the Christmas season. So she'd been hired full-time for six weeks, at his doctor's recommendation. The opportunity she'd been waiting for.

She had a history with his family.

She tapped the doorbell again, but no one came. She knocked on the thick oak door and—

A blistering curse cut the air.

Another expletive reverberated, followed by a substantial splash. She gripped the thick wooden rail, looking around. The frozen pond out front was clear and unbroken. Thank goodness. Winters in Alaska could be treacherous.

More curses carried on the late-afternoon wind. Now that the shock had passed, she realized the shouts were most definitely coming from the back of the house.

She secured her grasp on her heavy purse and picked her way faster down the steps and along the slick walk. Her feet crunched through packed snow, trees creating an icy arbor as she followed the voice to the back of the ranch-style mansion.

A glass dome covered a pool area.

She peered through the frost-speckled windows. Unable to believe what she saw, she blinked, and still the strange vision was clear as day.

A towering man with jet-black hair waded chest-deep in the water with his arm overhead to keep his cast dry.

It could only be her boss, Marshall Steele. Risking his cast—or worse yet, risking slipping into the depths—to save a dog.

Marshall inched closer to a scruffy little mutt paddling in panicked circles. Tally's heart squeezed in sympathy for the dog, her gaze drawn to the pup's unlikely savior. Time to quit gawking and act.

She prayed the side door of the solarium was unlocked. She tugged and—thank goodness—the sliding glass panes parted. "Hello? Can I help you?"

A gust of wind blew through the open door, rippling the man's discarded jacket by the pool, Stetson on top shuddering slightly.

He didn't answer, his focus on the dog. Maybe he hadn't heard her?

Rushing closer, she needed to help before he got the plaster wet. And the poor pup was gulping in water, growing more frantic by the second.

Tally tugged off her boots and slid out of her coat

before wading down the steps. "Hello? Let me get the puppy before you get your cast wet or slip—"

He glanced over his shoulder.

She almost lost her footing. His coal-dark eyes chased away the chill in an instant, sparking tingles of awareness. Such magnetism. Such mystery.

Such raw sex appeal.

It wasn't fair for one man to be that handsome and rich. His thick black hair curled ever so slightly from the water. He had impossibly long eyelashes and dark eyes with an exotic air. The hard lines of his body broadcast muscles earned the old-fashioned way and not through a gym.

This was her boss?

Heaven help her. Life wasn't fair sometimes. Given the secrets she held, the sensual draw posed a serious risk. But her need for peace with the past and a steady future insisted she hold firm to taking this job.

She shrugged off the unwanted attraction and focused on plunging deeper into the pool, wading, then swimming past him in awkward splashes as the warmed waters pulled at her clothes.

"Be careful," he called, his deep voice muffled by the water in her ears. "Don't get bitten."

She didn't bother answering. She hadn't thought about the scared canine biting an unfamiliar person. But the possibility didn't deter her. The pup needed saving, and her boss needed to keep his cast dry. Yet another twist on her imagined fairy-tale life. She did the saving these days.

Swooping an arm forward, she wriggled her fingers. And just missed the mutt. She heard more splashing behind her as her boss—Marshall—approached.

The dog's head dipped from sight. Panic flared inside her, followed by determination. She dived underwater and powered toward the sinking dog. She stretched her arms, making every inch count. She reached with both hands and sank her fingers into the fur, hauling the little fella tightly to her chest.

Kicking hard, she powered to the surface and extended her arms upward. The soggy scrap squirmed in her grip, gasping for air. Her feet found the bottom, and she started toward the shallow end.

Slamming straight into a steel wall of wet man.

Of course he couldn't have conveniently been some flabby octogenarian. Her boss was so hot, she half expected the water dripping from him to start steaming off his muscled body instead.

"Um," she stuttered, "excuse me."

"Nothing to excuse. You've saved the day." His low voice was as sexy as those muscles.

"Hardly." She eased past him. She'd worked too hard to nab this job to let wayward attraction derail her.

In sync, they sank back onto the pool steps, side by side, his thigh against hers.

"Thanks for getting Nugget," he said gruffly, taking the squirming dog from her with one hand. Not a puppy at all, but a full-grown small-breed dog. "Are you okay?"

"I'm fine," she said breathlessly, wondering why she didn't move away. "How's your cast?"

"Fine, no worries." His injured arm rested on the edge of the pool, the soaked mutt tucked under his other arm. "I appreciate your assistance out there. Nugget slipped into the pool as we were coming in from a walk. He got disoriented and couldn't find the steps."

This scraggly little brown scrap was his? She would have expected this man to have some large breed, a hunting dog maybe.

What other surprises did this Alaskan oil baron heir have in store?

"Glad to have been of service," she said.

"And you are?" He lifted an eyebrow, his gaze flickering ever so quickly over her wet shirt. Not lingering so long to be offensive, but just enough to relay interest.

And he didn't know who she was.

Awkward.

She should have realized... "I'm your new house-keeper, Tallulah Benson. People call me Tally."

His smile faded, and he stepped from the pool. When he stood, water dripped from his soaked jeans. Denim clung to one of the best butts she'd ever seen.

"Ah. Tallulah Benson. Right. You're the person my doctor and stepmother conspired to hire."

Conspired? His stepmother—Jeannie Steele— had implied she was merely helping him with the interview process. Tally rose, the enclosed area not as warm now that she was drenched. "I was under the impression your arm limits mobility for certain tasks." She cast an exaggerated glance at the shimmering waters. "Such as swimming."

"I would have managed," he said on his way to a set of shelves with stacks of folded towels. "Worst-case scenario, the cast might have needed to be replaced."

"No doubt you would have been just fine." Provided he hadn't slipped. "But you don't have to manage. Are we going to stand here and catch pneumonia while we argue, or am I hired?"

"Hey, I'm sorry to be a bear." He pulled a tight smile, flexing his hand at the end of his cast. "I know this isn't your fault. You're just doing your job."

"So happy we're finally on the same page about my working here."

"For six weeks. But just so we're clear, I'm not incapable of taking care of myself." He opened a large cabinet and pulled a towel free, wrapping up the shivering pup.

"Understood. And I'm not a nurse. I'm here to clean and cook for you." She grinned, crinkling her nose. "And save your puppy."

The glimmer of humor in his dark eyes sparked a hunger deep in her belly. She'd been so busy working the past couple of years to make ends meet, there'd been virtually no time for dating, much less something more intimate. Not that it was a possibility with her boss, especially not *this* boss. She was holding on to secrets about her father's role in his family's tragedy.

"Please help yourself to the towels. I would get one for you, but I'm limited these days."

She reached past him for the fluffy terry cloth, more to shield herself than to dry off. Her breasts were beading with awareness, much to her embarrassment. Hopefully he would chalk it up to the cold weather. She prided herself on her professionalism. She might not be from an oil-rich family like him, but she was proud of her work. Of the life she'd built all by herself.

Life hadn't been as easy for her as it had been for Marshall Steele, born with money and good looks.

She hugged the plush towel.

An awkward silence fell between them, a truly inauspicious start to her first day on the job. This man—his well-being—was a part of her job description.

"Are you all right? Did you get your cast wet or slip before I arrived?" she asked. "We should get you checked out by the doctor."

"You're not my nurse, remember?" He tossed her words back at her. "And you don't look anything like a Tallulah."

He'd been expecting someone more…formal perhaps? There wasn't much she could do about that right now. But she would earn his respect with her job performance. "Well, I guess that's why people call me Tally." She smiled. "The service said you'd asked for live-in help over the Christmas season while your arm heals."

"Live-in?" He tossed aside the damp towel and

wrapped a fresh one around the dog. "I was expecting day service."

"It's a long drive from town, especially if the weather's bad, which is typical this time of year." She struggled to keep the panic out of her voice, her teeth chattering. "I was told there would be room and board included."

"My stepmother overreached. Just because she's been married to my father for a few months doesn't give her the right to schedule my life."

A cold knot started in her stomach. Tally had heard rumors that things were strained blending families when the Steele patriarch had married the widowed matriarch of their business rivals, the Mikklesons. The news had been full of bumps in the road as the Steeles and Mikkelsons merged their companies into the Alaska Oil Barons.

Tally needed to make him understand her need to stay here. "I've already sublet my apartment to an older couple from Kansas who want an extended Alaskan Christmas."

"Sounds like you're in a pickle."

His dismissive tone set her teeth on edge. This wasn't a game to her. This position was crucial to her finally putting her past to rest. She needed to keep the job, and she didn't have the disposable income to just find another place to live. Never again would she be flat broke and vulnerable.

"I signed a contract. It clearly states room and board are included."

"I'll reimburse you, and you can stay in a hotel."
And still he hadn't opened the door into the house.

Someone as wealthy as Marshall Steele couldn't
possibly understand what it felt like to have no one
to depend on, no options.

"Your stepmother will be upset." She searched
for the right tone to persuade him to go along with
Jeannie Mikkelson Steele's plan. "She seems like a
very caring person with your best interest at heart."

"And she's your boss."

"No. Actually, you are my boss."

"If I let you stay." His half smile encouraged her.
And enticed her.

She hugged her towel tighter around herself. "We
can debate the details later. Right now, it seems there
are more pressing matters at hand. Such as caring
for the dog and finding dry clothes." She held up a
conciliatory hand between them. "Can we please
table this discussion until we're both in dry clothes?"

His eyes flashed with heat again, just a hint, that
awareness staying in the respectful realm while
still flattering. "Fair enough." He nodded toward
the door. "Follow me and I'll show you to a guest
suite. I assume since you planned to stay, you have
a suitcase."

"I do." She rushed to add, "And please don't insist on getting it. It won't look good on my résumé
if you break your other arm."

He chuckled, but his jaw had a stubborn set. "If
I let you carry your own luggage, I'll have to sur-

render rights to my Stetson. You can hold Nugget while I get your things out of your car."

He passed the dog to her. Without another word, he disappeared outside in his wet clothes. She cuddled the little dog—some kind of tiny terrier—close. Her boss was a stubborn one, all right. She would do well to remember that and tread warily. Surrendering on the suitcase issue seemed wise. She secured the towel around the shivering dog and cradled him like a baby.

Working for anyone in the oil-rich Steele family would prove to be a boon in more ways than one. She could pad her résumé in a way her previous jobs hadn't provided. And being with the Steele family could give her the opportunity to somehow make peace with her past. She desperately needed to find resolution for how the long-ago tragedy in Marshall's life had eventually led to her own father's suicide. He'd been her last living relative, other than a newborn baby she'd given up the next year.

How surreal that her life, her past, was so entwined with this man's. Not that he or his family even knew who she was. And she preferred to keep it that way for now. As far as they knew, she was just the temporary maid service.

But she was also the daughter of the drunk airplane mechanic responsible for the death of Marshall's mother and sister.

"Nugget, it appears our quiet bachelor-pad lifestyle has suffered an invasion," Marshall Steele said to his scrappy little mutt, currently sprawled on the bathroom floor, clearly savoring the heated tiles.

Easing the arm of a T-shirt over his cast, Marshall couldn't stop thinking about the new cleaning lady who would be living under his roof for the next six weeks.

He preferred the solitude of his ranch home, or of recreational time spent riding and reading. Solitude was something the rest of his overlarge family didn't seem to understand. The cleaning lady was the latest in their well-meaning attempts to help him. He'd thought their insisting on the holiday charity fundraiser being held at his house was a rather heavy-handed way of interfering with his social life. But sending a sexy woman to live in his house for the next six weeks was definitely going overboard.

And yes, he was grouchy as hell after taking a tumble at the end of a rodeo ten days ago, breaking his dominant arm in two places. The cast and sling left him barely able to dress himself. He was stuck wearing shirts a size too large so he could wedge his cast through. Thanks to one ill-timed kick from a horse, he couldn't even manage to save a ten-pound mutt from a paddle in a pool.

A mutt currently drifting off to sleep, unimpressed with anything Marshall had to say.

He worked the button fly on his jeans, trying to keep his mind off images of his new housekeeper in her suite changing into dry clothes, too. Images of her sleeping under his roof at night.

Having her work days here helping prepare for

the upcoming fund-raiser to be held at his home would have been somewhat simpler to manage than having her be his damn babysitter. But it wasn't fair to penalize her for his family's overreach.

Which left him with a dilemma.

He believed her when she said she'd sublet her place to save money. And she was correct that his stepmother—and therefore his father, too—would be upset if Marshall rejected help recovering. But Tally was a significant distraction.

He kept a rigid control over his world now, a far cry from his partying years full-time on the rodeo circuit. He'd played hard—drunk hard. Too hard. He'd been sober now for four years. Not a minute of it easy, but then taking it one day at a time was part of the program.

He should have known better than to step back into the rodeo ring, even for a onetime special show. For an instant, he'd been distracted by demons from the past, and now he had a broken arm to show for it.

As well as the knowledge it could have been much worse if that hoof had caught him in the gut or head.

He needed to get his focus back and his life reined in again. Holidays were difficult enough with the stress they brought, but with his recent accident… He was in a vulnerable place. He needed to steer clear of any temptations that could derail his sobriety.

He picked up the phone and dialed his father. "Dad, you and I need to have a talk."

Jack Steele chuckled on the other end. "About what?"

"I'm not sure what agenda you and Jeannie have going on, but it's not going to work." The two were inseparable. Marshall found it tough to believe his father wouldn't know about the new employee. He snagged his socks from the top of his dresser and sat on his king-size bed.

"You'll have to give me more information. I'm in the dark."

Marshall thumbed the phone on speaker with a frustrated sigh so he could tug on his socks one-handed. "Just because so many of your kids are set-tling down doesn't mean I'm interested in joining the ranks of the duly domesticated."

"So you keep telling us," his father answered. "And what does this have to do with Jeannie?"

"I agreed for her to hire a part-time housekeeper. Not a live-in Victoria's Secret supermodel."

His dad laughed again, louder this time. "Son, I don't see why the two are mutually exclusive. Seems that would be politically incorrect and downright wrong to factor looks into the hiring equation."

Something was up. He just didn't know what. "Did Jeannie interview the prospects?"

The line went silent.

"My point exactly."

"So the housekeeper's that attractive?"

Understatement. Her red hair, perfect curves and personality full of grit had sparked a fire in him.

"Well, it didn't help that she was starring in a wet T-shirt contest when we met."

His father spluttered on the other end of the phone. "Run that by me again?"

"I was in the pool fishing out Nugget—"

"Whoa. Hold on. You were swimming with your cast on?"

"The dog fell in, so to call my rescue efforts 'swimming' is a stretch. Besides, I kept my arm above the water." He tugged on gym shoes. Even putting on his boots was an ordeal.

"That was damn reckless," his father said softly. "What if you'd reinjured yourself, worse this time?"

"Then I would have gotten patched up again. I couldn't let Nugget drown. You would have done the same."

A low grunt carried through the phone line. "True enough. How did the pup end up in the pool?"

"We were coming in from a walk," he said, casting an eye at the scraggly pup who had come into his life when a member of his AA group had moved to Europe, "and Nugget ran through the sunroom door full tilt straight into the water."

"Then the new hire showed up?"

"Exactly. Tallulah Benson's got spunk, I'll give her that." He couldn't shake the memory of seeing her plunge into the water, determination firing in her hazel eyes. And for heaven's sake, how was it he remembered her eye color? "She jumped in, pushed right past me and scooped up Nugget."

"Ah, thus the wet T-shirt reference."

"Uh-huh." The revived image of her soaking wet with all those curves on display threatened to steal his focus clean out from under him. "I was worried about her getting bitten since the mutt was so freaked out by this point. But she handled things with complete calm and competence."

"She'll need it to deal with you."

"Are you insinuating I'm difficult?"

"Not insinuating. I'm stating facts. You're stubborn, which can be good when you have a task to accomplish and bad when it holds you back from asking for help." He paused. "I'm concerned about you."

There was something in his father's voice that gave Marshall pause. No one knew about his alcoholism. But had his dad somehow figured it out? Was the cleaning lady some kind of family spy to keep track of his sobriety?

The thought felt paranoid, but there was something reserved about Tally's sparkling hazel eyes, a hint of secrets…

Although who was he to judge? He had secrets of his own to keep from her.

"Dad, let's just say the position of the live-in cleaning lady is contingent upon my say-so and leave it at that."

No matter how intense the draw of his housekeeper, he was going to table the attraction for as long as she was working for him.

Two

Being drawn to her boss was not wise. At all.

But the laws of attraction defied logic.

She needed to get dressed quickly and start to work before her logic slipped further away.

Tally tugged on a soft long-sleeved cotton shirt—her work uniform along with khaki slacks. She just had to hold firm for six weeks. Surely she could keep her hormones reined in for that long.

She reached for her fur-lined ankle boots, her toes still chilly from her dip in the pool. Even the heated water had left her sprinting for her suite, teeth chattering.

Or maybe it was the man who'd sent her running, needing distance from her tempting boss. It was better to focus firmly on her job.

She'd cleaned a few upscale houses, but nothing like this. Her bedroom was more of a suite, larger than her apartment. No wonder room and board was such a big deal with this kind of accommodations.

Sure, she was proud of the life she had built and the place she called home. Everything in her apartment served a utilitarian purpose. This larger-than-her-lifestyle room felt antithetical to her experiences, but she couldn't deny the appeal. Floor-to-ceiling arched windows allowed natural light to pour into the space, washing the dark furniture in a luxurious glow. She scrunched her toes, taking in the sensation of the plush carpet as her eyes pulled to the view out the windows. To the sight of rugged Alaskan wilderness, tall pine trees kissing the sky. A mountain loomed in the distance, looking so impossibly beautiful that it seemed painted. Tally could have stayed in this room for hours, just watching the breeze set the shrubbery to life.

Unable to justify delaying any longer, she made her way to the kitchen to prepare dinner, taking in pine panes on the ceiling. As she moved through the sparsely decorated hallways, Tally felt like she was winding her way through a forest. The incorporated wood features, the natural color palette. It all felt like an extension of the outside world.

The Steeles seemed to have everything money could buy…and yet they'd suffered the worst blow a family could face, losing two loved ones. She understood that kind of pain wasn't anything money could fix. Her father had killed himself out of guilt for his role in that plane crash, and his death haunted her still.

She shook off thoughts of the past that threatened her focus. She needed to familiarize herself with the place, to do the best job possible so as not to arouse suspicion.

Like her bedroom, the kitchen featured a grand window over the sink, allowing another breathtaking view of the wilderness. The stone facade of the octagon kitchen island repeated the use of natural elements in the house. More stone framed the pine cabinets where condiments, spices and mixing bowls were carefully arranged. Laying a hand on the sand-colored granite countertop, she surveyed the rustic space. Light bounced off the glass cabinet panes. Built-in appliances were sleek and functional.

Perhaps she'd mischaracterized this space. Not quite a forest. The arrangement of stones reminded her of a special she'd seen on Viking halls. Something decidedly masculine about this space had her cheeks heating even though Marshall hadn't reappeared. She'd been given a list of her boss's preferences, courtesy of his new stepmother. What she hadn't known how to make, she'd studied up on prior to arriving.

The inside of his refrigerator was just as incredible as the rest of the house.

Stocked to the nines with fruits, meats and a variety of cheeses. The freezer was every bit as impressive. She hadn't even made it to the pantry yet, but she felt sure preparing meals here—and eating the food—would be a dream.

Cooking for Christmas in this restaurant-quality space would be memorable. She itched to get to work on researching menu options.

And yes, she was distracting herself with business to keep her mind off her boss. She wasn't sure what she'd expected. The Steele siblings were all renowned for being attractive and intelligent. She should have researched more about Marshall in particular, but she'd never come across this issue in her work in the past. She'd considered herself immune. She'd been wrong.

But more unsettling, it seemed to her, those rogue feelings were reciprocated.

There'd been a curiosity in his eyes that gave her pause. She didn't want him searching too deeply. She needed to keep her professionalism in place, do her job and lay family ghosts to rest. All so she could move forward with a future that was secure financially and emotionally.

"Tallulah…"

His voice pulled her out of her reverie.

"Tally," she reminded him without looking over her shoulder. She kept her head buried in the refrigerator to cool her cheeks, which were already heating with a blush.

"Tally…" His footsteps drew closer. "What are you doing?"

"I'm making you something to eat. Hopefully you'll share, because I'm starved," she said with a brisk efficiency she hoped would set the right tone going forward.

A tone that didn't involve the two of them soaking wet, inches apart.

"Ah, the whole room-and-board deal." He leaned a hip on the polished stone counter.

Tally did her best not to appreciate his rugged unkempt hair, which curled ever so slightly. Or the way his scruff highlighted his sharp, strong jawline.

"Exactly." She pulled out a package of ground moose and fresh vegetables for burgers. Not fancy, but fast and filling with top-quality ingredients. "Where's your dog?"

"Nugget's drying off in my bathroom, staying warm on the heated floor."

A heated floor for a pup. This was definitely a world away from her little apartment. Another reason the attraction to this man was dangerous. A romance between her and her wealthy boss was an unlikely match from the get-go.

"I took a guess at what you would like based on what was in your refrigerator and a list of favorites from your stepmother. Although some of what's in the fridge looks like meals brought over by others, perhaps to help during your recovery? You're lucky to have so many people who care for you." She tried to keep the wistfulness from her tone. She'd understood too well how difficult life could be without family support when she found herself alone and pregnant. Did Marshall appreciate the blessing of his big family?

"You've done better than I could have one-handed. Thanks." He gestured to an indoor grill with a chimney vent. "Although I can grill them."

"You could. But I prefer to earn my keep." She busied her hands placing the ground meat in a bowl to keep from surrendering to the temptation to pick a piece of lint from his shirt. To touch him.

"There's not going to be a lot to keep you occupied around this place." He passed her the fresh spices. "I'm fairly self-sufficient, even with the cast."

"No offense meant, but the place is dusty." In fact, she'd already made a list of tasks to accomplish before the fund-raiser and in preparation for Christmas. The holidays were going to be chaotic enough blending the Steele and Mikkelson traditions. Luckily, much of the Christmas prep would also double as party prep. She needed to stay focused on her work, her tasks and her goal of making peace with her family's past. "I don't know what you were paying the other cleaning lady to do during her visits."

"Are you angling to take her place permanently?"

His question caught her off guard. If her father hadn't been the mechanic for that fated aircraft… If she hadn't found her boss so incredibly attractive…

Then yes, this would have been the perfect job for her to seek long-term.

But that wasn't the case.

"I'm only pointing out facts. My work will speak for itself and hopefully garner a good reference for another job." She placed the patties out for the burgers, arranging three on a dish. "Wait until you see what I can do with my special brand of homemade fabric softener."

"Homemade, huh?"

"I use all-natural cleaning supplies. Better for the environment and my health." She'd started off mixing her own to save money and go easy on the environment, then found she liked the products better. She felt better, too—less sinus and skin irritation from work.

"Am I going to start seeing tofu and alfalfa sprouts in my food?" He tapped the plate, eyeing the burgers suspiciously.

"Do you like sprouts and tofu?" she found herself asking contrarily, even though they were both low on her list of favorites.

"Haven't tried them." He turned on the indoor grill, the flames licking upward to heat the grate.

"So you prejudge." She was playing with fire, bantering with him. Yet she couldn't seem to stop.

"Do you always argue with your employers?" He turned toward her to take the plate, their fingers brushing.

The light touch sent electricity crackling through her, leaving her loath to pull her hand from his.

"Not arguing. Just making conversation."

"Uh-huh." He took the plate, backing away slowly, then turned.

He flipped the burgers on the grill, the sizzling meat sending spicy scents into the air. His low growl of approval stirred her. Deeply. Calling to mind other primal pleasures.

Six weeks suddenly sounded like a very long time.

* * *

Heat built inside him faster than any smoking from the stone grill. Marshall watched Tally turn toward the pantry, all sass and sex rolled into one.

He read loud and clear the boss/employee boundaries she was keeping in place, and he respected her for that. And still...he was tempted.

Nudging the burgers on the grates and judging them nearly done, he knew full well there was no tofu or sprouts blended in since he didn't keep any in stock. Still, she'd made him laugh. Something he didn't do often.

Through narrowed eyes, he watched her arrange lettuce, pickle wedges and tomato slices on a small platter. She had a smooth way of moving, each motion blending right into the next.

Had they met a month ago, he would have pursued her like gangbusters. But with his broken arm and the taste for alcohol simmering just below the surface, he was reminded how tenuous sobriety could be.

He couldn't afford change, not now.

She set a lone place at the table.

And somehow it seemed to be making a bigger deal out of the attraction not to do the obvious and invite her to join him. "Tally, set a place for yourself, too."

She glanced at him quickly, worrying her bottom lip between her teeth before nodding slowly. "We should plan out my work schedule."

"Now?"

"If you're too busy watching those burgers—" she stared at him pointedly with those alluring hazel eyes "—then just let me know when would be a better time."

There she went, making him chuckle again. "Now's fine. Let's plan."

"Thank you. I need to let the hospital know when I'm available."

"Hospital?" he asked. Keeping up with this woman's conversational diversionary paths could make a man dizzy. Then he thought of her "all natural" quest. Was she ill? She likely didn't have much of a financial cushion to take time off.

He thought of his sister Naomi's teenage battle with cancer. Her return to health had been draining. He couldn't imagine someone managing such a major health crisis while working full-time.

Tally folded napkins alongside the silverware, deep red hair feathering down her back. "I volunteer in the NICU—neonatal ICU—holding babies that are there for extended stays."

A sigh of relief left him. He also wondered how he'd let himself jump to such a dire conclusion so quickly. This woman had him off-balance with her sexy confidence and curves to match. "Aren't their parents there to hold them?"

"The parents stay as much as possible, but they often have jobs or other children that make it impossible to be at the hospital twenty-four/seven. Touch is so important to any baby, and even more so for a struggling preemie building up their immune system."

His admiration for her grew. She had a fiery crusader's spirit to go with that fiery red hair. This was the kind of woman a man admired, the kind of woman a man married. And he wasn't in the market for happily-ever-after.

He would wager money she wasn't the affair type, even if he wasn't her boss. Even if this had been a month ago, even if his life wasn't teetering on the edge. His broken arm and the frustration from the restrictions of his recovery had him longing to pass the time with a drink.

The last thing he could do. He'd worked too hard for his sobriety. He picked up the small platter. "Keep your volunteer schedule in place. If you could just give me a copy, we can work around it here."

Her hazel eyes sparkled with appreciation. "That's very kind of you." Then the spark turned to something else. Suspicion, perhaps? "Don't think you're getting rid of me so easily. I'll still be working at least a forty-hour week for you."

"I'm sure you will," he said. She seemed as tenacious as Nugget. "There's plenty of flex when those hours can be, since I have business to attend to as well."

"Thank you." She wiped her hands on the apron tied over her khaki pants. "You're entirely too accommodating, you know. I would be a much tougher boss."

"And since I guessed that about you, there's no need for me to be a hardnose." He slid the burgers from the grill onto the platter. He'd always found, as one of the middle children in the Steele clan, there were better means for getting his way than the open bullheadedness of his siblings and father. "Well, unless you put sprouts in my burger."

"Message received, boss." She sliced fresh sourdough rolls, then gestured to the table. "Supper is served."

He held out her chair for her, his eyes meeting hers. The air crackled with awareness, so much for someone he'd just met, but undeniable.

Without question, the woman beside him was far more enticing than any feast, no matter how appetizing.

Cradling a premature baby girl in her arms, Tally still felt guilty for taking a half day off only twenty-four hours after beginning her new job. But Marshall had insisted he didn't care if she shuffled tasks into the evening and that he had a business meeting with his uncle, anyway. Having her out of the way would actually be helpful.

She suspected he'd made up the last part, but she had a list of tasks to accomplish after she finished at the hospital. Dusting was the least of her concerns for getting the house ready for Christmas.

Marshall's place could seriously use a woman's touch. She'd acknowledged that much in the cleaning she'd finished before she left for the hospital.

Toe tapping the chair into motion, she rocked with the baby girl—Stella Rae—mindful, always, of the monitors and tubes hooked up to the little one.

Despite the gravity of the NICU ward, despite the hardships these babies and their families all faced, the hospital staff went above and beyond. It came out in the way the nurses fussed, lingered past the end of a shift, and the pool of dedicated volunteers. Everyone who was part of this community dedicated time and emotion in ways that made it slightly better for the suffering families.

Which was why she smiled sadly at the Christmas decorations in the ward. The holiday wouldn't be the same for families struggling with a hospitalized child. But there were touches here and there, attempts to bring some normalcy, and yes, joy, to this ward.

A nurse in reindeer-themed scrubs with a Santa pin passed by Tally. A squat artificial Christmas tree twinkled at her from the corner of the sitting room, minor touches of Christmas cheer.

She had her work cut out for her on more than one front with Marshall Steele. Now that she'd started her job and met her enigmatic boss, she wondered what she'd been thinking.

How could she ever expect there to be peace over her father's role in the plane crash? Seeing Marshall Steele made the family feel so much more, well, real. Which should have been obvious.

Her plans to help them, to let them know her fa-

ther wasn't a bad man, had seemed so attainable before, and now? Far too simplistic.

Regardless, there was no backing out at this point.
She had signed on for the job, and she needed the
work. If an opportunity presented itself to discuss
the past, she would take it.

For now? Her best bet was to focus on the present, starting with the sweet weight in her arms as
she rocked back and forth, humming "Away in a
Manger" under her breath.

A door swept open, and a local social worker
strode through. Felicity Hunt had become her friend
over the past month. In the case of a child entering
foster care, a representative was assigned to stay
with the child at all times until the little one left
the hospital.

Working with Felicity recently had made Tally
revisit some of her own past. When she, too, had
sat in a similar position, with a baby of her own. A
baby she'd given up in order to ensure her son had
the best life possible.

Felicity made people feel comfortable as soon
as she flashed her smile. In her early forties, the
woman had a natural beauty and an effortless air
with her understated style. Her straight brown hair
was clipped back with a simple gold clasp.

Above all, her genuine kindness and caring radiated from her.

How different Tally's life might have been if a
woman like Felicity had been the one to guide her
through the lonely process of giving up her baby

for adoption. Or perhaps even help her find ways she could have kept her baby while building a secure future.

The what-ifs of such a scenario gut-punched Tally. She did her best to swallow the thoughts down, focusing on the fact that she did have Felicity in her life now. And for that, she was eternally thankful.

Tally had spent a lot of hours rocking infants alongside Felicity. They'd learned a lot about each other while cradling fragile little lives. Felicity had been in the foster care system as a child, changing homes frequently at first until landing with a wonderful family, where she stayed until graduating from high school. She considered them family still.

Tally admired her strength and how she'd powered ahead in spite of all the strikes against her.

The sleek brunette adjusted the hospital gown over her red sweater dress and scooped up a tiny baby boy, cradling him in her arms and settling into a rocker beside Tally. "Hey, friend. How's the new job working out?"

"My boss is very…accommodating." She eyed the fragile little boy in Felicity's arms and thought of her own son.

"That's rather vague." She raised a delicately arched brow. Felicity had a way of appearing cool and collected, ready for a board meeting, even with hospital wear tossed over her clothes.

"He has been completely flexible with my volunteer hours. But that could be because he really doesn't want me around." Could she have mistaken the interest in his eyes at the pool, and then again in the kitchen? "His family insisted on hiring me."

"Ah, he's an independent sort of man. That can be a good thing, you know." Felicity had shared her history of divorce from a spoiled mama's boy who'd lost job after job.

"True, but I found him walking into the indoor pool to fish out his dog."

"With a cast on." Sighing, Felicity shook her head and cradled the baby boy. "Males. I understand them better at this age, for sure."

"The dog was so small, Marshall probably could have gotten the tiny mutt out with the cleaning net." Tally chewed her bottom lip, remembering how frantic the precious little dog had been.

"But that would have been obvious."

And she could see he hadn't been willing to leave anything to chance. The pup was important to him, and she couldn't deny that touched her. "Luckily I arrived so he didn't end up in the deep end."

"You both were in the pool?" A slow smile spread.

"Not my most professional entrance to a new job, but it seemed wise at the time."

"Hmm." Her smile twitched. "How old is your boss?"

Tally stayed silent for a moment, unwilling to rise to the bait. Workplace romances? Nope. Especially not with this man. "Let's talk about your love life."

Felicity winced, tapping the rocking chair back into motion. "Point taken."

"Exactly. At any rate, my time's up here today. I need to get back and inventory the Christmas decorations to calculate how many hours to allot for setup."

"I wish some of my coworkers had your organizational skills," Felicity said, her lips thinning with exasperation.

The door opened with a clutch of doctors and medical students entering to conduct rounds, cutting off further conversation for now. Tally finished her volunteer shift, kissing the sweet Stella Rae goodbye before bundling up to head out into the December cold. She walked through the hospital, past the entries for a wreath-decorating contest, each one created by a different department.

What would her life have been like if she'd been able to train for a career field like Felicity's? Regrets were a luxury and waste of time. Holding her coat tighter around her in the chilly garage, Tally found her sedan and settled behind the wheel. She fished her keys from her purse, a mermaid charm dangling from the ring, a fairy-tale token her mother had given her as a child.

Three unsuccessful cranks of the engine later, she rested her head on the wheel. She'd prayed her old car would make it through another year. A repair would deplete what she'd managed to save so far.

And now, on her second day in her new job, she would be late returning. So much for impressing her new boss. She thumped the dash with her hands, tears close to the surface, as they sometimes were when emotions got the best of her after time with the babies.

A tap on the window pulled her from her self-pity. She looked up, surprised to find Felicity outside her car. Tally rolled down the window. "Yes?"

"Need a ride?"

A wave of relief swept through her. "If you don't mind terribly. It's forty-five minutes away, and that's if the weather and roads cooperate."

"I don't mind at all. It's a joy to do something for you for a change. I owe you for all those cups of coffee you've brought to help me through a long day." She nodded. "I'm parked over here."

Grateful beyond words, Tally gathered her purse and locked her car. She climbed into the passenger seat of Felicity's SUV, the heater blasting a welcome warmth.

"Thanks, Felicity. I really would rather not have to bother my new boss if I can avoid it."

Felicity's brows shot up. Tally could see questions dancing in those deep brown eyes. They'd shared a lot during countless hours rocking babies. But today, Tally had held back in discussing her boss, and she could see Felicity had picked up on that.

Keeping her friend's curiosity at bay had been tough enough in the hospital. It would be downright impossible to keep her attraction to her boss a secret from Felicity once he was right there in front of her in all his charismatic glory.

Three

Parked on the sofa in front of the fireplace, Marshall glanced at the window to check for Tally's sedan—for what seemed like the tenth time. What was keeping her?

He should have been able to lose himself in work today with his uncle. Conrad had been accommodating in coming out to the ranch so Marshall didn't have to deal with the seat belt around his broken arm.

Flames crackled in the river-stone fireplace, a blaze he'd started in anticipation of Tally's return. Where was she? Concern picked away at him even as he tried to lose himself in work.

The day had already begun to wane, the antlered chandelier providing a dusky yellow light as he and

Uncle Conrad continued talking through options for the company's newly formed charitable foundation. He'd signed on to the board, offering his accounting skills. He'd always been all about the quiet of crunching numbers, riding, hiking, the logic of counting steps and weighing odds.

Leaning back into the burgundy sofa, he rubbed his eyes. For the past several hours, he'd been staring at figures and documents on his tablet. Relentless strategizing, feeling the weight of the company's new image on his shoulders.

Of course, not all his thoughts lingered on the spreadsheets. Somehow even when Tally wasn't here, she managed to permeate the space with her personality. Even now, he found himself looking around his living room, his gaze sweeping up to the open-tiered second level—a reading nook complete with panoramic views, his place to unwind with a good book.

Had it really been as dusty in places as Tally suggested? The thought of his new, fiery employee also served as a distraction he could ill afford, especially now with his sobriety tougher to hold on to because of increased stress in his life.

Tapping the phone on his leg, he glanced at the security feed, since looking out his front window a dozen times now wasn't gaining him any traction. Still no sign of her.

He held back a sigh that would have caught his uncle's attention. To many, Conrad seemed like a happy-go-lucky sort, always rolling out the charm.

But he was more than that. He was the kind of person always there in a time of need. He'd been more than an uncle. He'd been a second father to the Steele children.

Especially after the plane crash.

The family had been stunned to its foundation by the accident that claimed the lives of Marshall's mother—Mary—and his sister Breanna. He, his father and his remaining siblings had retreated into a world of grief. Uncle Conrad, their father's brother, hadn't been a part of building the Steele oil business. He was fifteen years younger than Jack, and had been brought into the company after finishing grad school with an engineering degree. He'd been a part of the North Dakota expansion. The Steeles had started in Alaska and moved toward the Dakotas, and the Mikkelsons had grown in the reverse direction, each trying to push out the other. Looking back, Marshall was struck by the fact that his role in the family and in the business couldn't have been as easy as Conrad made it look. Perhaps they'd taken advantage of the fact he was a bachelor.

Turning the screen off, Uncle Conrad gestured to the living room, reading glasses spinning loosely in his hand. "I don't know where they found this new housekeeper for you, but I can already see a difference."

"And that's just from minimal time working before she went to the hospital to volunteer. She's a spitfire full of energy, that's for sure." He looked sidelong at his uncle, face tight as he remembered the way she'd flung herself into the pool to save his dog. From across the room by the floor lamp, Nugget stretched lazily, then moved to settle beneath Marshall's feet, head resting on his paws.

"Spitfire, huh?" He scratched his chin. "I'm sure she'll be a great help preparing for Christmas and the charity shindig."

Marshall grunted in response, his mind still filling with images of Tally soaking wet, every curve outlined and calling to his hands.

"Yeah, I'm on the fence about this whole bachelor auction."

"A bachelor auction?" He pulled his thoughts away from those tempting memories of Tally in the pool, memories that must be messing with him. He couldn't have heard his uncle right. "Please say you're kidding about them planning to parade us around on a stage."

"Wish I could accommodate you, but I'm afraid not. The publicity's already in the works."

"And you're participating as well?" He hadn't really given a thought to his uncle's single status. But Conrad *was* fifteen years younger than his brother.

He shrugged. "The money goes to charity."

Marshall's eyes narrowed. "I'll make a big fat donation instead."

"You're welcome to donate whatever you wish. But just so we're clear, if I'm hauling my old self on that stage, so are you." He set the tablet on a side table, careful not to move the bear statue.

"You're far from old."

His uncle dated widely, but commitment hadn't worked out well for him. One engagement had been broken off just shy of the altar. And Conrad's brief marriage had ended not long after his wedding on a glacier.

"Well, thanks for the sweet talk, nephew, but you're not going to distract me. You're expected to participate."

Marshall rolled his eyes, though he still hadn't given up on trying to get out of the bachelor auction. Tapping his phone screen again, he noticed a car coming up the driveway. Except it wasn't Tally's car.

On the screen, he watched as the passenger-side door opened. Red hair whipped in the wind. So it was her.

A stab of jealousy and disappointment flashed through him. He hadn't considered that she might already have a man in her life. And that thought worried the hell out of him, because it shouldn't matter. He shouldn't be thinking of her that way.

Then he realized he was thinking with his libido rather than his brain. Not cool. Something must have gone wrong for her to have gotten a ride with someone else. The weather led to too many traffic accidents.

Concern sent him to his feet as the front door opened.

Nugget lifted his head from his paws.

Tally took his breath away with her face pink from the cold. He lost track of how long he stared at her—and she at him—until his uncle cleared his throat and reached for the shopping bag of cleaning supplies she carried. Marshall then noticed the woman standing beside Tally. A lovely brunette, someone who might have caught his attention on another day. But right now, he only had eyes for a certain redheaded spitfire.

"My car died. I caught a ride with a friend." She gestured to the brunette holding another bag of cleaning supplies. "This is Felicity Hunt. She's a social worker who was up at the hospital for a case."

"Nice to meet you, Ms. Hunt." He crossed the room to take Tally's parka. The heat of her body clung to the well-worn jacket. Her crocheted mittens hung half out of the pocket. "You could have called me. You would have rescued me from plans of a bachelor auction at the Christmas fund-raiser."

"Bachelor auction?" Felicity echoed.

Conrad chuckled under his breath.

Tally tipped her head to the side, then said, "I handled getting home, but thank you for the offer."

Marshall's broken arm be damned, he needed to do something for her. "I'll send a tow truck and have my mechanic look at it."

Tally winced. "I don't want to take advantage. You can deduct it from my paycheck."

Marshall appreciated her independence, but the repair was a drop in the bucket to him. "We can discuss it later."

Conrad stopped alongside him. "Ms. Hunt, could we offer you supper to thank you for your trouble?"

"I'm fine, thanks. My workday started early, so I should head home."

Marshall nodded to the tall brunette. "That was kind of you to go out of your way."

She waved a hand dismissively. "It's not that far, but I should be going." Felicity turned to Tally. "I'll see you next week. Today was so busy we didn't get to chat much, and it seems we have, um, lots to talk about." Grinning, she jabbed her hands into her coat pockets.

Conrad grabbed his coat from the nearby elk antler coat rack, yanking on his overcoat. "I'll see you to your car."

Marshall looked at his uncle in surprise. Interesting.

Tally picked up both bags of cleaning supplies, bright red hair sliding forward over half of her delicate face. Backing toward the door, she took a deep breath. "I'll get to work now."

He usually enjoyed the solitude of his life. But he was restless and couldn't work that off with a ride. Ah, hell, who was he fooling? He'd been waiting for her to get back all afternoon.

"You've been volunteering since lunch. I thought you could use a break. I pulled a meal from the freezer and placed it in the oven."

She turned toward him, her eyebrows knit with… confusion? She assessed him a moment before speaking. "That's thoughtful. But I'm supposed to be taking care of you."

"I can take care of myself." Frustration made him

snap. Then he forced himself to relax, half grinning. "Although if you want to discuss giving me a bed bath, I'm open to the topic."

She lifted one eyebrow, crossing her arms under her full breasts. "That's most definitely not in my job description."

He scrubbed his jaw with his hand, awareness searing his veins. "You're right, and I was out of line."

"You're forgiven. And I'll gladly take you up on the supper."

"Glad to hear it."

"I want you to know I'll be washing an extra load of laundry to earn my keep."

"You're stubborn and prideful."

"I'm doing my job. And from what I was hearing your uncle say earlier, there will be a significant amount of company coming in for the holiday event. That means you do need me to get the house ready."

"Let's deal with supper first."

Having her here, living under his roof, was a major temptation when he was already on edge with wanting her. And even for a man who'd spent years of sobriety learning to resist enticement, he was feeling decidedly weak when it came to this woman.

Felicity Hunt had learned independence early on, first as the youngest child of a neglectful set of parents, then in the foster care system bounced from house to house. But she'd left all that pain behind when she'd accepted a job in Alaska fifteen years ago.

Still, even after all these years in the state called "The Last Frontier," she found herself parking in all the wrong places for getting stuck in the snow. Like now.

Her Texas roots were tough to shake in so many ways.

Snow settled in the crooks of Marshall's ranch mansion, coating the peaks of the roof in a thick blanket. In the glow of fading sunlight, the snow looked a bit like sand stretching on a beach. Temporarily, she felt transported to a lifetime ago. Far away from the rugged architectural aesthetics of exposed stone and wood. To Texas, a land of sunshine and buildings bearing Spanish influences.

A state where she never had to worry about her car getting stuck in an uneven patch of ice.

Smiling at Conrad Steele, she made a quick dash into her SUV, dodging the thick flakes of snow beginning to fall from the sky.

Turning the key over in the ignition, her vehicle roared to life. Buckled in, she laid her foot on the pedal. Prayed the car would overcome the ice.

No such luck. The car didn't so much as move.

Her cheeks warmed with a flush. Conrad Steele, who had been leaning against a post, his Stetson tipped down over his face, covering his salt-and-pepper hair, began moving toward her. Slow, determined steps.

Honestly, getting stuck in snow in such a short amount of time felt like a weird special talent. Though, as she looked at Conrad Steele's square jaw and those bright blue eyes, she wished this particular talent had manifested at literally any other moment. After her messy divorce, she was done with emotional entanglements. Her job was everything to her now.

He knocked on her window, an easy smile on his lips. "Do you need some help there?"

"I've been driving in snow for fifteen years. Thanks, though."

He nodded, taking a step back. But just one, she noted. He folded his arms, a movement that seemed to accentuate his broad shoulders.

Felicity willed her car to move forward. What was it that they said about the power of thought? If you wanted something bad enough, it would happen. Apparently, her car hadn't gotten the memo.

Rolling down her window, she locked eyes with Conrad. "Fine. Yes, I would appreciate a nudge."

His blue eyes lit with a roguish smile. "If you'll give me your number."

She stifled the urge to laugh, which would just encourage him. "Aren't you supposed to keep yourself available for some bachelor auction?"

"You're not making this easy."

"Somehow I think you're a man who's not interested in easy." She'd meant it as a simple statement of fact, and yet innuendo hovered between them as tangible as their foggy breaths. Her background in psychology made her all too aware of the power of Freudian slips. "Now can we please nudge my vehicle free?"

He laughed, a sexy, low rumble.

God, he was tempting. From his roguish smile to those broad shoulders. His breath from his laugh fogged the air between them, luring her closer. And for a moment, she considered testing the attraction.

For a moment only.

This man had the look and confidence of a player. And she wasn't one for games. She'd worked hard to build her life here, and she refused to let anyone unsettle that. She loved her job and hoped an opportunity would open soon for her to shuffle from the foster care system to a full-time position at the hospital.

After her divorce, she'd been determined to commit herself to her work, certain her ability to build long-term relationships had been permanently derailed due to her dysfunctional upbringing.

Her parents had struggled to make ends meet— tough to do when spending all their money on drugs and alcohol. Twice she'd gone into the foster care system when teachers had expressed concerns, only to be returned to the home where she slept under her bed.

However, when her father left her in the hot car to bet on dog races, the cops had found her, and that time, she hadn't been returned to her parents. The stress of bouncing around foster homes hadn't been easy, and in a strange, inexplicable way, she'd missed her dysfunctional family. But she'd also appreciated the regular meals, clean clothes, and lack of drug paraphernalia mixed in with her toys. Her messed-up childhood had made her too vulnerable, and she'd married a man who cared as little for her as her parents had. She hadn't even suspected his drug use until it was too late.

She'd learned well not to trust and wouldn't start now.

Bracing her shoulders and her resolve, she rested her hands on the steering wheel. "Thank you for the help. I should stop chitchatting and get on the road."

She made fast work of rolling up the window before gripping the steering wheel, ready—needing—to leave. Still, she couldn't keep her eyes off the rearview mirror to watch Conrad Steele climb in his truck. He drove forward slowly, his bumper nudging hers ever so gently.

Still, her stomach lurched far more than her vehicle for a man she'd only just met.

Loading the dishwasher, Tally couldn't ignore how much she'd enjoyed the simple dinner with Marshall.

With my boss, she corrected herself.

None of her previous jobs had included room and board. And more often than not, she worked through lunch to finish early. So she didn't share meals with others often, and Marshall was a surprisingly good conversationalist for someone reputed to be reticent. Perhaps people mistook his good listening skills for something more aloof.

She closed the dishwasher and couldn't help but notice how the stainless steel door reflected him working at the kitchen table. He had spreadsheets laid out and his tablet open, his broad hands sifting through.

Why did he insist on working at the kitchen table? He had an office. She'd heard all about what a solitary man he was. Jeannie Steele had warned her that she might need to coax him out of his "cave" to eat.

Tally slid a casserole dish into the dishwasher and shut the door on the half-full load. This man defied understanding on a number of levels.

The silence between them crackled like the sparks popping in the fireplace, drawing her toward the heat.

She worried her bottom lip between her teeth. Less comfortable silence between them might be a better thing. "What are you working on?"

"Ledgers."

"Ah, the Steele wealth." She winced the second she said it. Talking about money was, well, rude. Not to mention out of line since he was her employer.

"It's actually for the riding school I run. You're right in thinking I don't need the cash, but I enjoy it."

"A school for rodeo wannabes." She started the dishwasher. "Interesting."

"Actually, most of my clients are children. There are a few adults as well who didn't grow up in the saddle and want to learn."

He grew more intriguing by the moment, showing he was more than a sexy man with broad shoulders and a great butt.

"For an injured guy, you sure stay busy. Did you muck out some stalls one-handed, too?"

Keeping things light seemed the way to go with so much chemistry in the air. The way goose bumps raised on her arms every time he walked past. How the husky timbre of his voice made her heart beat faster. Her instincts said he felt the attraction, too, but there was a world of difference between *thinking* he reciprocated and openly acknowledging as much.

Leaving things unsaid maintained a wall she needed to continue her job. A job that offered financial security and, hopefully, some form of peace over her father's suicide.

He slid his papers together as snow piled up outside the window at a steady clip, moonlight reflecting off the pristine white. "And there's more to keeping this place going than riding horses."

"I do realize that." She spritzed the farm sink with cleaner, then sprayed water along the sides. "I didn't mean to come off flippant. I'm sure you miss it, riding horses, the school and the rodeo circuit, too, perhaps."

"Hmm." He waved dismissively, sliding the spreadsheets into a binder, then powering down his tablet. "Sure I do. It's my passion."

That last word launched tingles through her, her breasts tight and sensitive in her bra. She cleared her throat. "I'm sorry you're stuck in a sling."

He waved aside her sympathy. "Speaking of things we're passionate about… Tell me why volunteering at the hospital is so important to you that you'll use up your time off rather than relaxing like most other people would."

That was the last thing she wanted to talk about. No one in her life knew of the baby she'd given up for adoption. There hadn't been anyone in her life to share the grief with when it happened. And now? More than ever she wanted to move on. It was better to depend solely on herself.

Besides, the subject of her baby wasn't something a person just dropped into conversation. Although right now, she wondered why she'd never thought to share that part of her past with Felicity.

Tally turned her attention back to drying the sink and yes, giving her back to Marshall. "I like to help people. Guess that means I'm in a good job."

"There are lots of ways you could help. Why choose a hospital setting?"

The answer to that was so simple and complicated at the same time. She wiped her hands on the small towel slowly, turning back to face him carefully, keeping her features guarded. This man had a way of sliding under her defenses.

"I like babies, and I'm probably not going to have any of my own. So I love other people's."

He studied her with assessing eyes, a half smile kicking into his face. "You're like some kind of saint."

"Hardly." She'd made so many mistakes in her attempts to move forward with her life on her own.

"Don't you want anything for yourself?" He

leaned back in his chair, injured arm in a sling against his chest.

"A boss who doesn't go swimming in his cast?"

Laughing, he shook his head. "Fine. I understand. It's none of my business."

Marshall walked to the fireplace and pulled a poker from the tools. He stabbed at the logs, stoking the flames back to life again.

She wondered why he didn't choose a gas fireplace for ease, but then she was learning not to make assumptions about this man. Tally folded the hand towel and left it to dry in the sink. She walked to the table in spite of how much wiser it would be to leave for her room, to halt the temptation of talking alone with him. Of losing herself in the warm pools of his dark brown eyes. Of breathing in the fresh, outdoorsy scent of him.

Of seeing where this draw would lead.

"I didn't mean to sound rude," she said. It wasn't his fault her life had been difficult. But he was right that it also wasn't any of his business. She would simply need to set polite boundaries here. "Let's just say holding those tiny babies brings me great joy. I guess you could say I do it as much for myself as for them."

"That's really a special thing you've chosen to do. We should have you planning the charity event." Crossing back to the table, he tapped his closed tablet absently.

"Thank you, but I'm happy to do my own job well." She clutched the back of the chair to keep from stepping closer to him, risking brushing against each other.

"You know I'm not your boss, right? My stepmother is the one who hired you for housekeeping and holiday prep."

He watched her through heavy-lidded eyes, the exotic cast and dark color sending smoky curls of desire through her. She ached to run her hands through his tousled hair.

She gripped the chair tighter. "You're quibbling."

"I've been clear from the start that I find you attractive," he said without moving.

Boom. There it was.

The confirmation of mutual attraction. She wasn't fooling anyone with her boundaries. Chemistry between them was an undeniable truth.

She didn't have to step closer to steal a kiss. The knowledge that they both wanted one hung there in the air so tangibly she could almost feel his mouth on hers. Her body hummed with want until her breasts tingled again; a need too long denied gathered at her core.

The lure between them was potent.

So much so, it drew her feet—drew *her*—closer to him.

Four

He wasn't a monk by a long shot, but Marshall couldn't remember when he'd ached this much for just a kiss. Tally stood a simple arm's reach away, beside him at the kitchen table. Close enough to touch, to hold, to haul against him for what he knew would be a kiss to remember.

If she weren't his employee, he wouldn't hesitate to grip her shoulders and draw her to his chest. He didn't need the actual kiss to know that their attraction was combustible.

Maybe if he put the feelings on hold until after she finished working for him and his cast was off...

Except this giving, genuine woman who rocked sick babies in her spare time... She was dangerous. She was the sort who could crawl under a man's skin and into his thoughts. He couldn't forget his need for control of himself because of his history with alcohol. He was used to attractions he could manage, and this felt deeper. Like something that could rattle the control he needed to maintain now more than ever.

He skimmed his fingers along the top of her hand gripping the chair. She bit her bottom lip, swaying closer.

"Tally," he said, his thumb stroking once, twice before he squeezed her hand and pulled back. "Thank you for your hard work today. It's tough for me to admit, but the extra help will be welcome with the holidays."

Her shoulders braced, and she became professional again. "Of course. That's what I'm here for. Thank you again for the time off to go to the hospital today. I'm going to fold laundry before turning in for the night."

Unable to tear his eyes away from her, he watched Tally walk away. The sweet curve of her hips held his gaze and made him ache with thoughts of taking her up to his bed. Thoughts of exploring her body and discovering what made her sigh with pleasure.

But if he intended to keep his hard-won self-respect—and he did—he needed to keep his hands to himself. He walked a fine line these days and needed to keep it that way. Tougher to do on some days than others. And today was one of the toughest. Marshall rubbed along his cast over his aching arm.

His mouth watered for a taste of Tally as much

as it watered for a drink. An out-of-control feeling he couldn't risk.

No matter how much he wanted her, if he didn't hold on to his sobriety, his life would be worthless.

The next morning, Tally stifled a yawn behind her wrist as she stepped into the storage room, her eyes gritty. But she wanted to get an early start cataloging the Christmas decorations and discussing with Marshall what he wanted where.

She was finding it tougher than she'd expected to sleep under the same roof as her boss. The thwarted kiss had given her such dreams through the night—awake and asleep, her body ached with unfulfilled desire. He wasn't the kind of man one forgot easily.

And spending the day discussing holiday festivities wasn't going to help her rest any better, with the scent of him imprinting itself in her memory.

He was sexy and thoughtful and more than a little mysterious. Although she had secrets of her own to keep, and serious issues to put to rest.

Though Marshall's eyes were usually unreadable, holding a sultry mystery, his storage room provided a surefire way to get to know the man behind the smolder. High windows allowed bright white sunlight to settle on the shelves. Tally peered into the various containers, taking a mental inventory of his stockpile of supplies. It looked like he needed more fishing gear, judging by the depleted tackle box. Tally would make sure she ordered that—as a part of her job, of course.

She could best serve the house when she had a sense of how things were stored. As silly as it seemed, Tally could tell a lot about a person from their methods of organization and storage. This always seemed like a backdoor entrance into the minds of her clients. Once she understood the patterns and system of a particular house, she became more efficient. Learned what was most valuable.

And she couldn't deny, the need for that knowledge was especially intense around this man. He intrigued her, and that was dangerous. He was the last person she should get involved with. Perhaps she was seeking to learn more about him to find reasons *not* to like him. That would certainly be helpful.

She hauled her attention off the man and back to the task at hand. If she intended to keep this job, she needed to *do* her job.

Today's excursion into the storage room had a specific purpose—the transformation of the house into a winter wonderland. To make this place enchanting, Tally needed to see the decorations.

Reading from an inventory list could only spark her imagination so much. She'd always been the visual sort.

A green bin with a clear lid beckoned her; maybe it was the way the light splintered over it. Tally glanced into the box. Christmas ornaments and decorations were in neat arrangement. She looked at the row of green boxes with clear lids, all of them full of Christmas decorations. Pieces of Marshall's past.

More than a little curious, she pulled the first box

off the shelf. Opening the lid, she gently touched the carefully arranged decorations, so much more orderly than the hodgepodge storage from her childhood. But she'd treasured those all the same, looking forward to every year when her mother would add another fairy-tale ornament to her collection.

Feet shuffled behind her. A quick glance over her shoulder made the breath catch in her throat as her so-very-sexy boss wandered into the room.

An easy grin passed over his lips, sparking those bright eyes to life and making Tally's heart pound as her body ached to be closer to his. He closed the distance between them, leaning over the box to finger a reindeer ornament. Spice and musk filled her nostrils as she breathed in, all too aware of the inches between them.

Sleep wasn't going to be any easier tonight.

He lifted the ornament out of the box. "We're an outdoors kind of family—camping, riding, kayaking, fishing. Even in the winter. And the winter's amazing because there are even more things to do, like skiing and ice-skating."

He shot a glance to his cast, annoyance flaring in the way his jaw flexed.

Picking up a horse-and-cowboy ornament, she nodded at his healing arm. "Patience. You won't be in that cast forever."

"I'm counting the days until it's off."

She shot him a grin, looking over at him through her lashes. "That eager to be rid of me, are you?"

His hand returned to the box. She couldn't help

but notice the way his fingers lingered on an elaborate ornament, a kayak sporting a father and a son with fishing reels. The ornament appeared smaller in his broad palm as he examined it for a moment before he spoke again. "You've proven to be quite indispensable around here already. As you've noted before, this is a big place that hasn't been getting the proper attention."

"Is that a permanent job offer?"

And if it was, why did that possibility unsettle her?

His eyebrow arched, a twinkle of mischief in his eyes. "Is that an acceptance?"

Even if she could take his offer seriously, she couldn't imagine herself staying here and remaining just an employee. The chemistry was too strong.

She was better off holding firm to her plan for short-term employment in hopes of finding long-term peace. "You're just speaking out of holiday generosity. Besides, your stepmother hired me."

He slid a bin from the bottom shelf and pulled off the lid.

She smiled her thanks and sat on the floor beside it, looking at the hand-carved wood nativity scene. She tugged her phone from her jeans pocket and pulled up a Christmas playlist. Instrumental classics with a jazz twist softly filled the room.

Creating an unmistakable intimacy.

She was careful to keep an arm's length between them. She picked up the cradle, considering where she'd put this beautiful piece. Perhaps by the mantel? Above the stockings.

It was too easy to imagine what it would be like to decorate for a family—for real.

"What were Christmases like for you growing up?" she found herself asking in spite of her better judgment.

"Noisy. Busy. Much like this one will be here. We lived here then." He peeled back another lid, a whiff of cinnamon wafting free from leftover potpourri. "Dad believed in bringing us up with down-to-earth values."

"Does everyone usually meet here?" Would they be comparing what she put together with Christmases past?

He looked down, his thumb rubbing over the kayak ornament. "We grew up here. Once Dad built the new place, I opted to keep this place going, expanding the stables with a horseback riding business and stud farm."

"And even though this is your home, they're using it as a staging ground for the bachelor auction."

And he would no doubt be a main attraction. She clenched the plastic bin, holding back the urge to trace the line of his bristly jaw.

He rolled his eyes, a defeated sigh huffing free. "The bachelor auction wasn't my idea. But I'm just doing my part to support the family business."

"You got guilted," she guessed.

"Pretty much," he confirmed with a wry smile. "It'll be good to have you here to help. Although of course you should have Christmas Eve and Christmas off to spend with your own family."

His words chilled the heat stinging through her, bringing thoughts of her father. Of how her first Christmas after his death she'd stayed in a bad relationship rather than be alone. Of her child celebrating Christmas without her.

"I don't have family to visit. All the more reason I'm perfect for this job. I can see you through the holidays until you have full use of your arm."

"No family at all. I'm so sorry." He squeezed her shoulder lightly before sitting on the floor beside her.

Her breath hitched, and it took her a moment to gather her thoughts enough to reply.

"That's another reason why I work holidays. It keeps me busy, and also makes it possible for other workers to be with their relatives."

Did he know their legs were brushing? The heat of him breathed through denim, sending a tingle of awareness through her. This was much easier without his "help."

"You're welcome to join us. I don't expect you to work on Christmas Day. We're not helpless. Everyone will have their dish to make, and we're expected to pick up after ourselves. You can be a part of the festivities. What's your signature Christmas dish?"

What he described sounded…perfect. Normal. And not hers. "I don't want to be your pity case."

His gaze shifted off the decorations and slammed into hers, the air crackling between them. Instrumental music filled the silence, the room small and intimate, the world so very far away right now.

"Trust me, when I look at you—" his eyes flamed with a molten warmth "—pity is the last thing on my mind."

That heat flowed through her as she searched for words other than how much she wanted him. "Marshall—"

He held up a hand, shaking his head. "I shouldn't have said that. I think the holiday's messing with my head. Christmases aren't the same these days."

"Change is inevitable. You're all adults now, moving forward with your own lives."

"It's more than that. My mother and one of my sisters died in a plane crash. Holidays tend to bring reminders."

And just that fast, the desire in her cooled with the mention of why she'd come here in the first place, to find peace over her father's suicide. Except she wasn't the only one who'd been hurt. Would knowing about her father make things worse for them? Was her search for peace a risk to them if they discovered her reason for being here?

She would have to sift through all of that later. Right now, she could see only the man in front of her, a man in pain.

Touching him for comfort didn't seem wise for either of them, so she opted for silence, encouraging him to keep talking while she listened. Having a person to unload on was a gift she didn't take for granted. The loneliness after her father's suicide had been deafening. Her father hadn't been able to bear the aftermath of the plane crash that had taken the lives of Marshall's mother and sister.

How had Marshall been able to bear those losses?

Marshall continued, setting down the kayak ornament and picking up a mare-and-foal decoration made from jade. His fingers wrapped around it, white-knuckled. "Not too long after they passed, my sister Naomi got cancer. Our focus turned to surviving."

This room full of holiday memories suddenly felt so very sad and overflowing with pain. While Naomi had been struggling for her life, Tally's father had slid deeper into drinking until finally... she'd lost him for good.

Her voice rasped with all the unspoken hurt. "I'm sorry for all your family's been through."

"Naomi and Breanna were twins, so near to my age, sometimes people thought I was the twin, or that we were triplets."

"You had a close relationship." She'd read so much about his family, but there were nuances the news articles didn't cover.

"Yes, we all were, actually."

"Were close?"

"Well, we all stayed in the area, but things were never the same." He put back the ornament and swiped a hand over his face. "I didn't mean for this to become about me. It's Christmas. We're here. There's a party to throw to kick off the family's charity foundation. That's what matters."

She thought about steering him back to talk of his relatives in the hopes of learning something about the accident that could give her the answers, the closure, she sought, but his face was closed off. Shielding grief.

And if she pushed too hard, he could well shut down to her permanently.

Tally searched for the right way to strike the lighter tone he seemed to seek. "Even though that party means you have to be a part of the bachelor auction?"

"Even though." He cricked his neck from side to side and opened another bin of decorations. "What about your family Christmas traditions?"

The last thing she wanted was to discuss her family's tense holidays, with her father drinking his way through the season, growing more morose by the ounce as he ruminated about the crash. So she said simply, "My mother and I had a tradition where we picked out a fairy-tale ornament every year. I still have the mermaid one as a charm on my key chain." Just thinking about her parents made her throat clog. She needed to steer the conversation away from her past, fast. "You didn't actually tell me about your Christmases growing up. You just talked about winter overall."

"Isn't Alaska in somewhat of a perpetual state of Christmas once the snow falls? It is home to the town of North Pole, Alaska."

"I can see your big family making a trip there."

She leaned back against the shelves, unable to resist the lure of his deep voice.

"You guess well. We made a pilgrimage there every year. Dad said he would take us as long as there was one of us who believed in Santa Claus."

"Your brother Aiden is quite a bit younger than you are, isn't he?" She rushed to confess, "I read up a little on your family tree before taking the job. Just what could be found through Google, mind you. I only wanted to be prepared."

That was better to admit than having scoured the internet for information on his family out of a sense of guilt over what her father caused because he'd had a few too many drinks on the job.

"You're a professional, I can see that." He crossed his hands over his chest. "And back to Aiden... He pretended to believe until he was ten. He did an excellent job fooling our father."

"That's really sweet." She soaked in the light streaming through a high window, catching on the waves in his dark hair.

"Don't underestimate my little brother. He was charging my sister Delaney money to keep up his pretense."

"Why would she do that?"

He studied the moose ornament in his hand. "She said it made her feel closer to our sister and mother."

"Traditions have a way of keeping our loved ones alive." She thought of how much comfort she took from a simple ornament on her key chain. "I'm sorry you've lost so much."

He angled closer, placing the ornament back in the storage bin. "As have you."

If she breathed deeply, her chest would brush his, and that prospect made her tingle all over. She swallowed hard and forced words out. "Thank you."

"I can see the loneliness in your eyes." He tucked a lock of her hair behind her ear.

"That's not something many men would admit." Was that breathy voice hers?

His hand fell away and he moved back, giving them both the boss/employee distance again. "Don't give me too much credit for sensitivity. It comes from reading horses."

He paused, his eyebrows pinching together before he lifted his cast arm. "Although maybe I should rethink my ability to read people given my rookie mistake with a horse."

"I suspect it could happen to anyone. And as sorry as I am that you've been injured, I'm glad to have the chance at this job."

"This job shouldn't steal your whole Christmas season, though." He angled closer. "You should join in our plans."

"Um, I'm not so sure that's a good idea."

"It's an excellent idea. You deserve to have some fun." He straightened. "As a matter of fact, why don't you join us this Friday when we go see *The Nutcracker*? We can grab dinner beforehand. It'll be a low-key way for you to meet the family in person before they all start piling in."

She couldn't help but be curious to learn more

about them, to see how closely they resembled what she'd discovered reading up on them. What was real and what was paparazzi fodder?

"That's very generous of you to offer."

"Consider it my Christmas gift to a great employee."

"I've only just started."

"And look at how much you've already impressed me." He eased to his feet and clasped the doorknob. "I'll see you at lunch. Don't work too hard."

Before she could answer, he left, closing the door behind him, leaving her alone with the holiday music and boxes full of Steele memories.

Had she really just agreed to go out with him? But it wasn't a date. Just a boss offering his employee a ticket to a show.

So why was she already planning what she would wear?

Who had he been fooling that it didn't mean anything inviting Tally to join in their family's plans? Going out with her for dinner and the ballet on a Friday night felt exactly like what it was.

A date.

At intermission, Marshall's family milled about, visiting with drinks in a private room reserved for major donors to the theater. Boughs of holly and pine hung from the dark wood banister in the dimly lit room.

At the large red-cloth-covered buffet table with a spiraling candelabra, Marshall opted for spring water. At what point would his family notice he'd stopped drinking anything with alcohol in it?

Beside him, Tally sipped her champagne. He wasn't sure how he had made it through dinner without alerting his whole family that he had the hots for his cleaning lady. Temporary cleaning lady, he reminded himself, as if that might somehow make the attraction more acceptable. Not that his family had questioned his showing up with her. But he knew there would be talk among them once the evening was over.

Tally slid her hand in his, the softness of her skin stirring him. He shot her a curious glance, and she smiled, pulling him aside to show him a Christmas display in a window across the street. She arched up on her toes, bringing their heads side by side as she described how she wanted to re-create the look at his place.

He should be paying attention to her words, but he was so focused on the soft sound of her voice, the feel of her skin.

She squeezed his hand lightly. "Look at that snowman. Wouldn't it be fun to have something like that greet the family as they arrive?"

But it was all Marshall could do to stand so close and not pull her into his arms. He closed his eyes and breathed in the scent of her and imagined them together.

"Marshall? Do you like it?"

"Yeah," he said, his voice gravelly. "It's great."

She laughed softly. "You're not even looking."

He opened his eyes, and she was already walking away. A good thing. Because without question, the attraction was getting deeper, and this was not the time or the place.

And even if they were alone? Holidays were a dangerous, emotional time for him to risk a new relationship. He was on edge enough with his broken arm and Christmas bringing back memories of his mother and sister. In the past, he'd lost himself in alcohol over the holidays…

His family hovered around; Marshall's Uncle Conrad lifted a number of festive-inspired canapés on his plate and winked at him from across the well-decorated refreshment table. Marshall shot his uncle a dark glance. To his credit, Conrad simply gestured to the wasabi shrimp with avocado on rice crackers.

Blaring trumpets reached a subdued apex as the soundtrack from *The Nutcracker* played in the background. Holidays as usual.

Or almost as usual.

Marshall glanced at the woman beside him. Tally was stunning in her black lace dress. Simple, covering all the way to her neck. But formfitting in an understated way that drew his gaze like a magnet. Her hair was piled on her head in a loose topknot of curls, leaving her neck exposed as she leaned to listen to his sister Naomi.

The women hooked arms and walked toward the ladies' room. His sister Delaney followed.

Jeannie glided over to him, her floor-length red gown settling around her like the robes of a great monarch. A queen. "I'm glad to see that Tallulah is fitting in so well. That will make the holidays run all the more smoothly."

The rest of his family and the Mikkelsons went silent, all eyes on him. So much for keeping things low-profile.

He cradled his spring water. "She's efficient."

Jeannie gave a polite, knowing smile. Crossing her left arm to the crook of her right elbow, she let the champagne glass dangle in a relaxed grip. "I'm glad you acquiesced to having her around while you recover."

He quirked an eyebrow. "Did I really have a choice?"

His stepmother chuckled, raising the champagne glass to her lips, eyes wide and sparkling with mischief.

His brother Broderick slung an arm around his wife Glenna, softly twirling her hair between his fingertips as they talked to Trystan and Isabeau Mikkelson. Nearly everyone was paired up and expecting a baby. Marshall could see where inviting Tally might have been stirring rumors. That needed to stop. And the best way to stem that tide would be to ignore them, since it was unlikely a protest would be believed anyhow.

Jack Steele made his way to his son, a confident swagger in his worn-in black boots.

Marshall held up his hand. "Don't ask."

"I wasn't planning on it." His clapped him on the shoulder. "How's the arm feeling?"

"Annoying."

"Well, thank you for humoring Jeannie about the help around the ranch. It means a lot to her that this event go off without a hitch."

"About the bachelor auction—"

"You're already on the program. Jeannie and I feel passionately about starting this charity foundation as a tribute to her former husband and to your mother's memory."

Words rose in Marshall's throat with a feeling he didn't want to name. Wasn't sure if he could. But he knew he had to give it a shot. This was no scarier than riding a horse. Just had to do it. "Dad, all those Christmases when we were kids..."

"Yeah?"

"How do you keep them from overwhelming the now?"

His dad glanced at Marshall's water, then back up to his face. "It's not always easy. For those tougher days, I think about what they would want for me. And if that doesn't work, then I flip it around to what I would want for them if I were the one who'd gone down on that plane."

"That makes sense."

"Your mother would be proud of you."

Tipping back his water glass in a room of twinkling Christmas lights, Marshall wished he had his father's confidence in that, because no way she would have applauded the alcoholic he'd become. And if he fell off the wagon?

He wouldn't be able to forgive himself.

* * *

Tally had never been in a ladies' room quite like this. Posh velvet sofas, floor-to-ceiling framed mirrors and a red damask rug made the waiting area to the restroom feel like a spa retreat. An attendant stood patiently by, ready with warmed towels and other necessities.

She tried not to appear too wide-eyed at the luxury, but it was tough being blasé about such wealth.

Naomi perched on a velvet sofa, bracketed by carved reindeer. She cupped her cell phone, FaceTiming with her smiling baby twins—Anna and Mary—who were resisting going to sleep. Their coos echoed from the phone.

From a pearl-encrusted clam-shaped bag, Delaney retrieved a tube of dusty-pink lipstick. Parting her lips, she refreshed her color, pursing her lips together. She glanced over her shoulder. "Everyone else is being diplomatic, Tally, but I'm dying to know about you and Marshall."

Tally paused washing her hands, her mind filling with that tingly moment at the theater when she'd realized Marshall was breathing in her scent with his eyes closed. "There's nothing to tell. I work for your brother. He was polite enough to invite me along tonight in the interest of sharing the Christmas spirit since I'm away from home."

Delaney closed her makeup and put the tube back in her purse. "He hasn't participated in the Christmas spirit much lately."

"But he's having that huge holiday fund-raiser

at his property." Tally took the hand towel from the attendant, smiling her thanks.

Naomi's eyes danced with mischief. "We didn't leave him any choice," she said to the women while waving to her babies on the phone. "We wanted to make sure he stayed busy and didn't get crazy ideas about skiing with his broken arm. Besides, it's Christmas, and that's our childhood home."

She wasn't sure how someone would have given him no choice, but clearly whatever they'd done had been successful. The party was officially in the works.

"Marshall mentioned spending holidays there. I've started cataloging the ornaments to plan for party decorations. There are so many amazing family heirlooms."

"You're cataloging all of them? That's quite an ordeal. I don't think everything's been out in...well, I don't know how long."

Delaney nodded as she dusted bronzer powder along her face. "We've accumulated quite a lot of decorations over the years, I imagine. We lived there until some of us began university, then Dad built the new place, with private suites since we were getting older. It worked out well for living there after college while working for the company."

"It's nice you can still enjoy the place where you grew up."

Naomi waved to her twin daughters again before ending the call. "Marshall keeps the place in great shape. He's expanded the stables for the riding business." She paused. "It's really more of a charitable foundation. He makes his money off investments. He would have been a great investment broker—if it weren't for the fact that he hates office hours."

Tally's mouth twitched with a grin. "I've noticed that about him."

Delaney squeezed Tally's arm gently. "Whatever his reason for bringing you, thanks for what you did to get him here. This is a surreal Christmas for us with Dad's remarriage and the business merger."

"Everywhere I turn there are ads for the new combined family company, Alaska Oil Barons, Inc.," Tally mumbled softly.

Naomi sat on the sofa beside her. "Marketing has been on top of things, especially considering we had so little warning about blending the Mikkelson and Steele companies—and the families."

Tally toyed with the string on her handbag. "I'm no expert in the marketing field by any means, but the merger has appeared smooth."

Delaney leaned in. "My brother Broderick's romance with Glenna was rekindled when he went to see her about rumors causing stock market fluctuations. They went to confront her mom—Jeannie— and stumbled on Jeannie showering with my dad."

"Oh my." Tally clamped a hand over her mouth. "Um, I'm not sure what to say."

Naomi nodded, tucking her phone into her beaded bag. "That's pretty much how we felt when we heard about it." She rolled her eyes. "But Dad let us know in no uncertain terms that they were in love and getting married. We could get on board with it or move along."

"They certainly seem happy." So much so it almost hurt to watch them, knowing her own life was so lonely.

"They are happy and in love," Delaney said. "And they should live their lives as they wish. It just would have been nice if they could have eased us into learning about their relationship with a couple of dates first."

Tally scratched behind her ear. "I can see how the shower would have been a shocker."

Naomi leveled a steady look their way. "Thank God, they had time to grab towels—or at least that's what my oldest brother—"

"Broderick?"

"Right. That's how Broderick tells it. I can't believe you manage to keep all our names straight. There are so many of us now I feel like we should pass out a family tree to all newcomers. Maybe laminate or frame it for future reference." Naomi gestured to a framed *Nutcracker* poster on the wall, drawing a laugh from the other women. "Having Christmas in our childhood home will hopefully make all of this—I don't know—normal somehow? Sort of a 'fake it until you feel it' mentality."

Three peals of bells poured through the speakers in the ladies' room, overpowering the old-time Christmas tunes. Three minutes until the ballet resumed.

Butterflies pirouetted in her stomach over the simple prospect of sitting next to Marshall again on their non-date that felt remarkably real. Tally had taken this job to make peace with the entwined tragedies of their pasts, not to fall for him. But with each day that passed in his employment, it got tougher and tougher to remember.

Five

Who was he fooling?

Marshall figured it was time to stop lying to himself. This evening with Tally at the ballet was a date. Or at least he wanted it to be. He was attracted to this woman...*mind-blowingly* attracted.

Leaning against the counter at the coat check and valet station, he handed his numbered card to one of the young men with a curt nod. One attendant grabbed keys, while the other excused himself to collect coats from the hangers.

Absently nudging a cluster of gold reindeer on the far end of the marble counter, he listened to Tally talk to Felicity. Even the soft timbre of Tally's voice sent his mind whirring.

Itching to have her alone, he drummed his fingers on the counter, eager for the valet to hurry the hell up and bring his car around. Audience members filed past in a brush of gowns and winter capes.

Felicity buttoned her cape at the neckline. "Tally, thank you so much for sharing the extra ticket with me." She paused, looking over her shoulder toward the twinkling Christmas tree at the far end of the lobby. "And for arranging transportation. I've had a lovely time."

Tally gestured to Conrad. "Actually, it was Marshall's uncle who secured the box and limousines for us."

Marshall gathered Tally's wrap from the coat check. He'd chosen to drive his SUV. It had seemed practical at the time. Now he accepted reality. He'd wanted to be alone with her for the drive rather than sharing her with others more than he already had to at the show.

How had he become this drawn to her this quickly? Especially since she was risky, the kind of attraction that could get under his skin and not let go. He'd always been a far more methodical man.

Except when he'd been drinking.

Felicity tugged on her leather gloves. "Your uncle doesn't strike me as a supporter of the arts." She winced. "That came out wrong. I'm sorry. I only meant that the Steeles seem drawn to outdoor recreation rather than this kind of grandeur." The social worker gestured to the grand lobby full of jeweled patrons and crystal chandeliers.

Stepping closer, Marshall held up Tally's wool

cape. "We are. But the ballet is a family tradition going back to when we were kids."

Tally swept her auburn hair free of her cape, the silky hair rippling into place in a curtain he wanted to touch, to test the texture between his fingers.

To see it splayed over a pillow.

Smiling, Felicity held her silver clutch to her chest. "You're kind to include me."

"Well, our circle is expanding." To put it mildly. He reached in his own coat pocket, feeling for his sobriety coin, reassured by the cool metal. Hell, anything to ground him and not make him seem too interested in Tally.

Tally looped her festive red scarf around her neck twice. "Felicity, I'll be right back. I see the parents of a child I rocked last year."

As Tally walked away, quiet descended for a moment before Felicity said, "She is an amazing individual."

"I haven't known her long, but I agree." Very much so.

She turned her full gaze on him, pinning him with an unmistakably protective stare. "Handle with care."

This was not a conversation he wanted to have, and certainly not one he wanted Tally to hear. "As I said, I haven't known her for long."

Felicity laughed softly. "You know what I do for a living, right?"

Marshall wondered where his big, nosy family

was when he needed them to interrupt. "You're a social worker for children."

"I'm a social worker *and* a licensed counselor," she said with a knowing grin. "I read people for a living. And you're not fooling me. In fact, I would wager you're not fooling the others, either."

He was saved from answering by the limousine arriving to pick up her and his uncle. A blast of cold winter air blew through the open door as they left. With each bracing breath, Felicity's words sank in a little deeper. Maybe she had a point.

He was attracted to Tally, and she felt the same. In reality, he wasn't her boss. She was aware of the distinction, too. They both knew his stepmother was her actual boss, having interviewed and hired her to make sure the holidays and fund-raiser went off without a hitch.

If she wasn't *his* employee…perhaps that was the answer.

They would be going their separate ways after Christmas. Emotions and long-term entanglement didn't need to come into play. He wouldn't drink, but he would have her.

Time for a serious talk—about not being serious.

Conrad clasped Felicity's hand, easing her into the limousine. Just the two of them. Alone. Finally.

He settled into the black leather seat. Christmas carols filtered through the limo speakers. Luckily, Felicity hadn't commented on the fact that no one else was along for the ride to her place.

The rest of his family—and extended family—had departed, taking different cars to different destinations.

Felicity's cape fell open, revealing the red dress that hugged her curves. Her emerald green wrap brought out the golden flecks in her eyes. Dark hair swept up into a chic updo of some sort, feathery wisps framing her elegant face and calling to his hands to cup her cheeks, to taste her mouth.

But he could see the reserve in her eyes still.

He was a patient man. So he simply allowed himself to enjoy the view.

Tonight had given him the time with her he'd hoped for when he'd offered the extra ticket to Tally. No doubt about it, he'd wanted to ask Felicity out since the day he met her, but she hadn't looked open to passing out her phone number when he'd helped her get her car out of the snow. So he'd begun planning the right time and approach to woo this fascinating woman. Somehow, he didn't think she would be won over by grand gestures of wealth. But she had appeared to enjoy the ballet.

His desire for her ramped up. Already he could imagine the affair they could have. No strings. Short-term. Just two professionals enjoying explosive chemistry.

Conrad peeled off his gloves and stretched an arm along the back of the seat, Christmas lights outside twinkling as they drove through the capital city. "Would you like some sparkling water? Or champagne?"

She swept back a stray lock. "Water, please, thank you."

Did she know she was playing with her hair? Given her career skills reading body language, she had to know she was sending off sensual vibes.

Conrad reached into the mini fridge and selected sparkling water for Felicity before sitting beside her again.

She smiled, looking through her lashes at him. "I hear I owe you a thanks for the amazing seat and intermission party tonight."

"You owe me nothing." He passed her the small bottle of sparkling water as the limo pulled away from the theater. Their hands brushed, heat rising between them. "Attending *The Nutcracker* is a family tradition."

"And you always have the intermission party?" She sipped slowly, her lips a pale pink that drew his gaze.

He focused his attention back on her eyes. "That was my gift to the family this year, expanding the experience. You may have noticed that our family is large and growing fast. It would take just about all year to shop for everyone. So I planned this instead."

And yes, he'd had to pay a small fortune to purchase the extra seat with theirs, but it had been worth it to have her join them tonight.

Her eyes flickered over him, assessing. "Sounds to me like you're downplaying your role in orchestrating this. It's an incredibly thoughtful thing to do for your relatives."

He stayed silent. He wanted to pull his weight being a part of the family, but was also aware this was his brother's family. Conrad had been married briefly, and almost married once. He'd thought he might one day have kids of his own when he was engaged. After his engagement had ended just shy of the altar, he'd opted to stay single and enjoy being an involved uncle. All of which was too much to tell this woman he wanted an affair with. She was sexy as hell.

Which also didn't sound like the right angle for a pickup line.

The driver maneuvered through the well-lit town. Conrad had grown up here, and somehow the lights in the main square never ceased to fill him with something that felt a lot like hope. His mother and father had taken their family to the annual lighting ceremony every year. Always dressed in a puffy black parka, his mother had instructed him and Jack to make a wish the moment the lights powered on.

While he hadn't made it to the lighting ceremony this year, he still found a wish on the tip of his tongue as they passed holiday lampposts.

His eyes flickered from the scene outside, back into another source of light. Felicity leaned forward, a question forming on her lips. He touched the furrow in her brow lightly, the dim lights of the car casting a warm glow across her face. "What?"

She shook her head. "Nothing important."

"Try me."

She narrowed her eyes, a smile playing with her

lips. Those eyes sparkling. "I'm wondering whose idea it was for me to come—in the interest of thanking the right person."

The more truthful the better. He had a feeling if she sensed he was playing with the truth, then he wouldn't stand a chance. "I offered the extra ticket to Tallulah, hoping she would ask you."

"Hoping, huh?"

The limousine turned, the bumps in the road causing them to jostle closer together. "You make quite an impact, lady."

"Are you flirting with me?" Sipping her water, she watched him through her eyelashes.

"Absolutely." And he could see he'd made progress with her, but she wasn't at the point where she would accept. The chase was on. "Go out with me."

She gave a low laugh. "With an eloquent request like that, I'm amazed you're still single."

A light chuckle escaped him. A genuine one. "I'm known for being one of the more charming members of my family. Yet you have me at a loss for words."

"I think there may be a compliment in there somewhere."

"I hope so."

She turned from him, eyes focused outside the window to the falling snow. "Thank you for the request, but I'm taking a break from dating to concentrate on my recent promotion."

"Congratulations," he said before pressing on, "Then let me bring lunch to your office. You have to eat."

Her mouth twitched as she faced him again. "I eat in my car driving to and from home visits or on my way to the hospital."

That half smile playing at her lips spoke to him louder than her words. "You're playing hard to get."

Her chin tipped. "I don't play at anything."

His arm along the seat, he traced over the back of her neck, her silky hair catching on his calloused fingertips. "If you're not interested, then I'll take you at your word."

She hesitated an instant too long.

"So you're interested." He smiled inside as well as outside.

"Another time in my life, perhaps," she conceded, eyes turning wistful. Distant. As if she was analyzing something far away from the limo, the backdrop of Christmas lights.

Somehow that concession gave him pause more than if she'd said no flat-out. "You're really that focused on your job?"

"I have the opportunity to help so many more children."

The passion in her voice was so intense it took his breath away.

"You're making me like you even better." He ached to kiss her, and more.

The limo pulled up outside her town house, and he couldn't help fantasizing about how this evening could have ended. Perhaps could end someday in the future.

The chauffeur opened her door. She started to

step out, then looked over her shoulder. "Meet me in the cafeteria tomorrow at noon. I have a half hour free."

Victory pulsed through him. "I'll strive to make it a memorable thirty minutes."

She raised a delicately arched brow. "That's what I'm afraid of."

Tally wanted to hold on to this magical night until the very last second.

Her weather-resistant, heeled black boots crunched in the new-fallen snow as she followed Marshall along the covered walkway up to the ranch house—his garage was full. The familiar constellations were covered by thick clouds. Snowflakes tumbled through the air, collecting in her hair, melting on her cheeks.

Marshall opened the door, warm yellow light beckoning them inside. Stepping out of the cold, she crossed the threshold. Nugget wriggled and jumped, a furry bundle of frenetic excitement. The little dog let out a bark that sounded a lot like hello.

She shrugged out of her cape, the holiday glow of the night still lingering. Riding back together had been so...intimate, somehow. Like they were a couple. She searched for a safe topic. "You have an amazing family. You're so incredibly lucky."

"You fit right in." He took her wrap, his hands brushing hers as she passed it to him, leaving a tingling trail.

"It was an idyllic Christmas outing."

"And the season's just beginning." He draped her

cape over the back of the sofa and crossed to the fireplace. "Is there some holiday tradition you would like to include? I hate to think we're hijacking your whole Christmas."

The last thing she wanted was to talk about the holidays she'd had with her father passed out on the sofa. "I don't have traditions other than shopping for ornaments with my mom, so it's fun seeing yours."

He started a fire and then adjusted the flames. "If my arm weren't broken, we would have a lot more outings here to enjoy."

"Such as?"

He gestured to the two chairs bracketing the fireplace. "Other than horseback riding? Snowmobiling, skiing, ice-skating."

"Those sound fun." She sank into the overstuffed seat, tugged off her boots, then wriggled her toes in front of the fire.

"You should take your pick of any of those things. I can sideline coach if you need help."

How was his glance over her feet so sexy?

"Thank you, but I'm not here for a vacation." She straightened. "I'm here to work."

"That's between you and my stepmother." He sat across from her, leaning forward.

The flames cast shadows across his face, but the heat in his eyes was unmistakable.

She ached to angle forward and meet him halfway. He stirred something inside her that no one else had. And during the holiday season, it was tougher than ever to be alone.

But she couldn't afford to succumb to temptation. She needed this job…and she was keeping secrets, too.

Watching Tally walk away the night before had sucker punched Marshall. He'd felt it too deeply in his gut, wanted her too much. So much so, he'd come to his senses and realized he needed help.

He'd called his Alcoholics Anonymous sponsor, then he'd gone to an early-morning meeting.

Now, full of coffee and resolve, he found himself driving to see his oldest brother. Broderick, his wife and their daughter lived at the family compound in a large suite in the mansion Jack Steele had built when they'd outgrown the ranch house.

Set on a lake, the massive Steele family compound was picturesque. The bulk of Marshall's family lived here now, but he'd never felt like it was home. Not like the ranch, where his family had been whole. Except he wasn't ready to go back there and spend more time with Tally until he had his head on straight.

Marshall was struck again by how much his older brother, Broderick, resembled their father. Stetson tipped forward, he looked every bit the cowboy. Classic dark looks for a classic man. Turning the corner from the stables, Broderick made his way toward him. Christmas lights glowed in the dark Alaskan winter morning. His brother waved and shouted a greeting.

Marshall met him halfway. "Do you have time for a walk before you head off to work?"

"Of course. Glenna and I are working from home today, so my schedule's flexible."

They moved toward the water, picking their way around a tall, skinny pine tree. Boots crunched into the freshly fallen snow. Marshall wished they could ride instead. The weeks couldn't fly by fast enough until his cast was off and he could de-stress with a day in the saddle. Although that would also mark Tally's departure from his life.

Or maybe uncomplicate things?

Hell, he didn't know.

He glanced at his brother, the dock lights illuminating their path. "How's it going with building the new house? I've been meaning to stop by to see the progress."

"Slow but steady. Even though this place is as big as a castle, it'll be nice to have our own home." There was an edge to his voice. He scrubbed a gloved hand along his jaw, then said wryly, "Although we'll sure miss all the on-site babysitting for Fleur. She's a precious handful."

"At least you don't have to parade around in the bachelor auction," Marshall offered up.

"True, but I had a near brush with appearing in a Santa suit."

Now that was an image Marshall couldn't envision, not even since his brother had become a father when he'd adopted little Fleur. "Seriously?"

"Dad vetoed the Santa idea altogether when he

heard we were the only two on the ballot to play Saint Nick."

"Vetoed how?"

"He reminded us—insistently—that it's an adult event, therefore no red suit needed."

"Logical argument. Although I think it's ironic he has been pushing the notion of him and Jeannie stepping out of the leadership roles in the company, but he exerts veto power." Jack and Jeannie were easing back from running the company to spend time on their new marriage. And that made sense on the one hand, but on the other made total chaos for the family by creating a power vacuum that still hadn't been settled.

"I brought that up," Broderick continued. "He said he and Jeannie plan to keep their focus on the charitable aspects of the family portfolio."

"That makes sense…if they'd staged the fund-raiser here instead."

"The catering staff would be tripping all over us." He angled a look at Marshall. "And if the party had been here, you wouldn't have met Tallulah Benson. I wasn't mistaken in the sparks between you two."

"Let's talk about the party," Marshall said quickly, then wondered why. Hadn't he come here to talk to his brother about her?

"I thought you hated talking about the party."

"I do." Which was another testament to how much he wasn't ready to talk about his attraction to Tally.

Broderick chuckled good-naturedly. "Fair enough,

brother. Fair enough. When are you going to get that cast off?"

"I'm seeing my doctor at the start of the week."

"Hopefully you'll have good news." Broderick clapped him on the shoulder. "Stick around and join me for something to eat before you go. And maybe you'll tell me why you really came here."

Opening up was easier for the rest of his family. Probably why they all had been able to live in this family compound together and he'd secluded himself at the ranch.

Alone was easier.

A couple of days without Marshall underfoot should have made her job easier, but there were reminders of him all over his house.

Like his half-finished glasses of water with lemon. His extra Stetson. And heaven help her when she made his bed and the scent of him engulfed her senses.

And then there was his little dog, currently trotting along beside her on her way out to the main barn, the older barn tucked in the distance. She wasn't sure why he'd been keeping to himself, but he had, citing work commitments. Which made sense. He stayed busy overseeing the ranch and livestock.

Her boots punched through the snow as she strode faster. She knew she might be pushing her luck risking crossing his path, but she had a job to do as well. She reached to slide the barn door, which had an oversize wreath hanging in the middle. Christmas lights framed the rooflines of both barns.

She'd been touring the place for more ideas for decorating and breakout space for the fund-raiser. The new barn posed an intriguing option. And yes, she'd been keeping herself crazy busy in hopes of working herself into exhaustion.

Still, thoughts of how close she'd come to kissing Marshall filled her head. Along with a fresh wash of fantasies of what it would feel like to follow through on that impulse. And guilt about how she hadn't been honest with him about her father.

As she moved into the barn, a chestnut horse let out a low whinny of acknowledgment, and the scent of clean hay greeted her. She stared at the horse, who bobbed his head from side to side. Looking over her shoulder, she saw Marshall emerge from the tack room. The first time she'd seen him in two days.

Her breath hitched in her throat, and her stomach did a flip. Lord, he was too handsome, so ruggedly appealing it wasn't fair. Nugget barked a greeting, racing circles around Marshall's feet before sprinting over to dive into a pile of hay.

Trailing her fingers down the stalls, she wrestled for professionalism. "How did your doctor visit go?"

He'd left her a note on the kitchen table about the appointment.

"My arm is healing on schedule. I may even get the cast off by Christmas Day. Although that feels mighty far away right now." He looked down at the cast, frustration visible in his cheeks, a line of tension working from jaw to temple.

"That's good. But you don't look happy. What's wrong?"

"I was hoping to get rid of the sling—" he lifted his arm slightly "—and go to a smaller cast."

"I'm sorry." She could see how much it bothered him.

Aggravation radiated from him in waves. He reached into his pocket, fishing out some sugar cubes. "It is what it is. There's nothing I can do to change it."

He moved toward one of the stalls, extending his palm flat to the same chestnut horse who whinnied earlier.

"You're a good patient to realize that."

The horse ate the sugar cube happily, licking his palm. "Being noncompliant will only make this last longer." A dry smile played with his lips. "That doesn't mean I can't be grouchy about it."

He was handsome—and charming.

And she was susceptible. "Grouch away."

Stroking the chestnut's neck, he seemed to lighten. Such a simple interaction. It was like seeing a whole new side to him. "I wouldn't want to upset the horses."

She found herself drawn by the mesmerizing way his hand glided along the horse's chest. "They're that in tune to your mood?"

"Absolutely," he said without hesitation. He angled a steady look her way, his brown eyes so full of hidden depths. "How did your volunteering go this morning?"

His thoughtful question caught her unawares.

"It was quieter than normal." She'd rocked a fragile preemie whose single mom had to get back to work. The morning had been especially filled with reminders of her own baby and how hard life could be.

She'd missed the distraction of having her friend to talk with. She found herself reaching to stroke the horse. The animal lowered his head, the powerful muscles moving.

Marshall stroked, his hand moving alongside hers. "Do you ride?"

"I've never had the opportunity. It's an expensive sport." Even a quick survey of the barn showed it held more wealth than she knew what to do with. Leather halters with golden engraved plates. Leather lead lines. She could barely see into the tack room, but knew it held an array of saddles and bridles.

He nodded slowly. "True enough. But for me, it's not a sport. It's a way of life."

"I can see that."

He was at home here. That was obvious. Would it help her to understand him better if she shared something he enjoyed so much? The idea appealed more than it should.

Marshall tipped his head to the side. "How about you get on the horse since I can't risk it?"

The notion sounded enticing, especially when she

saw in his eyes how special that was to him. "But I don't know how."

"Lucky for you, I'm a good teacher." He dipped his head to speak soothing words to the horse. "Come on, Silk. I have a pretty lady for you to meet."

His voice and ease with the horse were mesmerizing. He slid a halter over the chestnut gelding and led him out of the stall. Clipping the horse to stall ties, he grabbed a basket filled with brushes.

Marshall's smile widened as he pulled out each brush, explaining as he went along. Her stomach knotted in tension and excitement, over riding the horse, of course. Not because the man was suddenly standing so close to her she could barely breathe. Right.

Hoping he wouldn't notice her nerves, she stroked Silk's neck.

"I'm going to tell you the biggest secret to riding." He winked. "Breathe. If you are calm, so are they. Riding is about constant communication between horse and rider. Blending your souls together."

His passion was evident as he spoke, and that fire mesmerized her until she hung on his every word.

"This is the pommel of the saddle, which leads into the horn." He pointed to the apex of the black-and-silver saddle. "When you're up there, feel free to hold on to the horn. You'll want to keep your weight centered. I'll explain more when you're settled in the saddle."

Placing a turquoise-and-black woven saddle pad on Silk's back, Marshall flashed her a grin. How did this man manage to turn her so inside out with a simple gesture?

He slung the bridle over his shoulder and adjusted the saddle pad. She reached to help him. Her fingers brushed his, igniting a spark inside her.

Marshall heaved the saddle onto the horse's back and adjusted the girth, his muscles flexing as he managed it one-handed. In a quick movement, he'd shucked the halter to the side, slid the bit into the horse's mouth and fitted the bridle. Nodding his head, a thick lock fell over his head, the hint of curl in his hair from the snow calling to her fingers.

She'd made a big mistake coming here, into his world, and thinking she could be unaffected. Thank goodness it was time to head outside, where the breeze could tease away the earthy scent of him.

Tally rushed out ahead of him, waiting, drawing in a couple of steadying breaths of icy air.

Stopping the horse, Marshall motioned for her to come over. "I'll help you up."

"I can do it." Her voice sounded foreign to her own ears, nerves getting to her. Besides, she wasn't sure her defenses could withstand the helpful touching that might be involved if he assisted her.

"I'll stand by. Just in case."

She nodded, hand going up to the horn. All she had to do was pull herself up. How hard could it be? She attempted to put her foot in the stirrup. With a great heave, she tried to hoist herself into the saddle.

Instead of forward momentum, she lurched backward toward the ground. But rather than crashing into snow-covered earth, she slid back into a hard-planed chest, turning in his arms.

Her breath hitched, and she could see he'd heard. His pupils widened an instant before his eyes narrowed. His arm banded around her, drawing her closer, and she couldn't find the words or will to stop this. It was just a kiss.

Just…one…kiss… Then so much more.

His mouth skimmed over hers, once, twice, sending a pulse of desire through her. The mere touch of his lips to hers had her melting against him, her hands twisting in the fabric of his shirt. He slid his wrist from the sling and wrapped both arms around her, pressing to the small of her back.

The hard-muscled wall of his chest was a wide expanse she ached to explore. Her fingers splayed wider, skimming under the leather vest he wore but over the flannel shirt. She looped her arms around his neck. It had been so long since she'd been with a man. But even that didn't explain the depth of her longing to be with *this* man.

He was so strong and thoughtful. But also mysterious in a way that intrigued her. Too much.

What was she thinking to kiss him this way? To lose sight of everything she'd come here to accomplish?

Regret stinging, she eased back, struggling for words to explain why this shouldn't have happened. Of course, she couldn't share those reasons, none of which should be spoken. The secrets she hid would only hurt him.

So she simply held up her hands and backed away from the greatest temptation of her life.

Six

Marshall had expected there to be fireworks once he kissed Tally. But he couldn't have imagined the explosive reality of having her in his arms. If the chemistry of a simple kiss was off the chain, then how incredible would sex between them be?

A thought he'd pondered through a long, restless night until he'd accepted that ignoring the attraction was only making things worse, deepening his craving. Perhaps the wiser move for his sanity and sobriety would be to pursue a no-strings affair with her, both of them understanding it was short-term.

Not that he planned to press that move just yet. He couldn't have missed that she was wary when she pulled away. And she'd been a no-show for breakfast, simply leaving muffins and fruit on the counter for him, along with a full coffeepot and a note. She'd spoken with his sister Naomi, and his family wanted to come over to help decorate this afternoon.

Damn, Naomi was pushy.

Still, he'd have a few more precious hours without his sister's well-meaning prodding.

His bare feet pressed into the wood floors that led to the living room. The place smelled of balsam and spruce from the pine boughs on the mantel and trailed around archways, but Marshall knew once his family arrived the greenery around the house would multiply exponentially. Holiday tunes played lightly on the whole-home speaker system. Marshall could see hints of Christmas already present, proof of Tally's quick, resourceful work.

The woman moved through her daily tasks with the determination of an Alaskan blizzard. Purposeful. Thorough. All-encompassing. And mesmerizingly beautiful.

Sitting on the leather couch's arm, he took a deep breath. Wondering the right way to navigate this space. He looked at the crackle of the fire, staring into the flames' dance.

A sense of being watched drew his gaze over his shoulder. Tally struggled with a bin, her white knuckles straining against a box that was nearly half her size. A pang shot through him, deep and true. Damn. Frustration rose in his chest that he couldn't alleviate the weight for her. Useless cast.

He took one side of the bin, irritated that he couldn't take the whole thing. Damn sling. "You should wait and let my brothers carry all of that down."

"So you got my note. I hope you're free?" She nodded toward the line of bins under a high window revealing a piece of the deep blue sky. They put the container down.

"I'm not sure I have a choice."

"You're the boss."

Was she reminding herself as well? "When Naomi speaks, we all line up."

Dressed in a bright red reindeer sweater, she shifted from foot to foot, tension heating the air between them hotter than the flames in the fireplace. "I should have checked with you."

He couldn't let her take the blame. "My *family* should have checked with me. But they went through you so I wouldn't say no."

"Why would you tell them not to come?" Her earrings, a pair of shiny jingle bells, chimed as she tilted her head to stare up at him.

He mulled how much to tell her. Being around Naomi was tough. Not her fault. But she reminded him of their sister Breanna. Brea had never reached adulthood, but if she had, odds were she would have looked like Naomi. More detail than he felt comfortable sharing.

"Holidays are rough when you've lost close family members. This one is especially rough." He leaned against the sofa back. "Only a few months ago a nutcase wrangled her way into the family busi-

ness and then made claims that somehow my sister
Breanna survived the plane crash."

"Oh my God. That's so cruel." Her legs folded,
and she sat on one of the bins marked "lights."

"Cruel or not, we have to look into it, which
dredges up the worst time of our life. The plane
crash was…horrific…" He swallowed hard, willing
back memories of his father sitting him and his siblings down to tell them. "DNA tests say my mother
and sister were on board." The pain of that time had
never dulled, but it had an especially sharp edge
these days with the current investigation into the
past churning up too many memories.

It didn't help that he couldn't use work to keep
himself busy, his ranch chores limited by the injury.
The past was too close.

And that increased the temptation to give in to
Tally and the forgetfulness he could find in her arms.

She leaned forward and rested a gentle hand on
his cast arm. "I'm sorry your family has to suffer
through so much—then and now."

How was it her touch radiated through plaster?
Damn, he was in trouble.

He hauled his focus back to the moment. "The
woman—Milla Jones—made the claim when we
caught her leaking business secrets. Then she disappeared somewhere in Canada. We have investigators checking into her past and working on tracing
her trail. Not that it will change reality."

"And your family has planned this big fund-raiser
at your place—and sent me here—to keep you busy

so you don't have time to think about the past since you live alone and are tied down by the injury."

"Seems so."

"I have this feeling I've made your life more complicated rather than simplifying things." She pressed her hands to her mouth for a moment before continuing, "About the kiss last night..."

And there was the root of the tension between them. This was the perfect opportunity to test the waters for moving forward with the attraction. "I don't want you to feel awkward or pressured. Anything that happened—or happens—between us is totally separate from your job here."

"That's kind of difficult. We're living under the same roof. Granted, the place is as big as a B and B." She winced, her words flowing faster. "Clearly, I find you attractive, but I didn't mean to kiss you. Acting on the attraction would make things too messy."

"Ah, so you find me attractive." He couldn't hold back his smile, or a pulse of pleasure over her admission.

She sighed in exasperation. "This conversation is not going the way I intended."

"Nothing between us has been predictable in the short time we've known each other." That was beyond an understatement. "Just think what else could be in store."

She swept her hair back with a shaky hand. "That only makes me more nervous."

The last thing he wanted was to make her nervous. "Are you sure I didn't take advantage?"

"No! Heavens no," she said with unmistakable honesty. "I worry I was the one who overstepped."

Ah, progress. He tugged a loose lock of her hair, testing the silky length between his fingers. "I promise, you didn't take advantage of me."

Her shoulders braced. "Don't laugh at me."

"I'm not. I think you're something else." He stroked the strand behind her ear before skimming a finger over the tiny jingle bell earring. "But I hear what you're saying. I won't kiss you again without your okay."

"You mean that?" she said in a breathy whisper that caressed his wrist as he pulled back.

"I do." He pinned her with his gaze if not his touch. He wanted there to be no misunderstanding between them. "Keep in mind, though, that doesn't mean I won't use other powers of persuasion. Because, lady, that kiss was one in a million."

Tally had relived that kiss in her mind again and again. Or more specifically, the memory replayed through her senses, every tingling detail as she helped decorate Marshall's home for Christmas. At least she had the distraction of a houseful of people today. His family was out in force to help. The sprawling living area was filled with Steeles and Mikkelsons, all in the holiday spirit.

As she had moved through the world, Tally discovered she had a knack for reading people, connecting with them. In the dark days, she liked to think it explained her ease with infants or how she'd settled on a career that required her to navigate other people's spaces with sensitivity. On the bright days, this extra sense afforded her the ability to make friends easily.

Shana, Chuck Mikkelson's wife, seemed to be one of the souls that beckoned to hers. The curvy blonde's gentle smile and infectious laugh felt familiar to Tally, like a home filled with sisters and sleepovers. A vision she'd always craved.

In the midst of Mikkelson and Steele family members, Shana felt like an extra-warm beacon. She'd helped Tally set out a fondue bar—a hot cheese concoction with veggies and breads—as well as a chocolate dip with fruits. In the middle, she'd placed gourmet pretzels to pair with either.

Carols piped through the sound system, jazz renditions of classic favorites. She wondered if her sexy boss knew how lucky he was to have so many people who cared about him.

Jack Steele had brought piles of live garland from a family cutting party, stacking the boughs neatly by the staircase. His wife, Jeannie, fastened intricate bows at intervals on the greenery. Elegant and classic, they would look stunning once they were strung. Tally couldn't help but be touched by this wealthy family who still took the time to decorate from scratch together.

Shana gripped a plate in her right hand, crossing the great living room to kneel beside Tally. Gathering her long skirt to the side, she settled in, blond hair in loose waves. Tally gave a small smile, arranging the nativity by the fire. She thoughtfully placed the animals, trying to capture the movement and sentiment of the story with the figurines.

Tally put the angel on top of the crèche. "You're all kind to come pitch in when you have your own homes to decorate."

Shana popped a chocolate-covered blueberry into her mouth. "I have a spouse to decorate with. The others all live piled into the mansion together. Marshall is here alone."

A roil of voices erupted from across the room as Broderick, Chuck and Conrad carried in a towering live Christmas tree. The fresh scent of pine hung in the air, blending deliciously with the warm cinnamon candles she'd lit an hour ago. Marshall followed behind, his face cross from not being able to do anything besides guide the tree toward its stand hidden in a massive decorative urn.

"I was hired to help him while he recovers." Not to make out with him.

"You *are* helping, and we're grateful to have found you. You've done a lot to make today all the more special." She lifted her plate of fruit drizzled with chocolate.

"All I did was haul down some decorations and set up a few snacks."

"What a great spread," Shana said, swirling a strawberry through the melted chocolate. Her eyes widened with delight as the chocolate coated the fruit. Truth be told, the strawberry looked mostly chocolate at that point.

"It's easy to put out a spread when the budget is virtually unlimited." As if Tally needed another reminder of their very different worlds.

"I hear you. I grew up with a more…limited… budget." Shana gestured to the massive living room. "All of this still feels overwhelming sometimes even though I've been a part of it for five years. But, of course, that could be because I don't remember the whole five years."

The statement fell flat. Pointed.

Tally gasped, at a loss for what to say other than, "Oh my. I didn't know."

"I assumed Marshall would have told you." Shana touched her forehead. "I suffered a mild aneurysm recently, and it left me with a patchy memory of the past few years."

"I'm so sorry. How scary that must be." Tally focused her full attention on the woman, abandoning the decorations.

"I'm grateful to be alive, and my memory is coming back in pieces. I have my health and my husband. That's so much more than I had before the hospital scare."

The men arranged the tree off in the corner, securing the live fir with a thin wire. Marshall nodded, looking pleased as he surveyed the way the boughs fell.

Tally stayed diplomatically quiet, not wanting to be pushy, but unable to squelch her curiosity about this family—Marshall's family.

Shana carefully picked up a crystal snowflake,

playing with the facets. "Chuck and I had a rocky marriage. We've found our way back to each other, and we don't intend to lose our way again."

"I'm happy for you."

"It wasn't easy." Shana exhaled hard. "I had a lot of insecurities to work through, and Chuck had a tough time balancing work with home life. We're both working on things, though. I have to admit, I sure didn't realize how much work went into a marriage, but I can't imagine my life without him."

"Sounds like you're an amazing couple." The love in their eyes for each other was unmistakable. It was hard not to envy that. Tally had felt so alone for so long, especially during her pregnancy.

"You're a good listener." Shana squeezed Tally's arm. "Thank you. It feels good to talk to someone who didn't know us before. It's like starting with a clean slate. That's a part of what motivated us to move."

"You're moving?" Marshall hadn't mentioned it. Tally couldn't imagine this family moving away from one another. "Where to?"

"To North Dakota, at the end of January. Chuck's taken a less demanding position with the company." Shana glanced at her broad-shouldered husband securing the towering Christmas tree. Her eyes shone with appreciation, love. Warmth and desire. "I know it wasn't easy for him to step back. There's a lot of tension between the Steeles and the Mikkelsons, power plays and such. That Chuck would do this for me… It means everything."

"You're a lucky couple."

"We've been given a second chance. Those are rare in life." Shana swiped an emotional tear from her cheek and smiled. "But enough about me. I want to know about you."

"There's not a lot to tell." Well, that was a lie, but there wasn't much Tally felt comfortable sharing with this family. "I grew up in Alaska. My mother and father passed away when I was still in my teens. I've been lucky to build up my cleaning clientele. I hope to hire on assistants within a year."

Shana smiled, then said, "Well, then the fundraiser is going to be perfect for meeting potential customers. Let's talk about plans, starting with that bachelor auction."

Tally listened while Shana talked about the different men in the family and some of their friends who would be participating in the event. The auction should bring in big money for their charity foundation.

For the first time, Tally really thought about someone purchasing a date with Marshall. She knew it was just in fun, but still the notion made her stomach knot.

She looked around for Marshall, realizing sometime during her conversation with Shana, she'd been distracted long enough to lose sight of him. Maybe that was her answer to how to resist temptation. Immerse herself in the holiday spirit.

And somewhere along the way, she would figure out how she was supposed to make peace with her past while not hurting this family that had already been through too much.

From the second-floor railing, Marshall watched Tally move seamlessly with his family, steering the decorating with an unassuming efficiency. Much the same way she kept the refreshments stocked, the fondue having been swapped out for a mix of gourmet subs made of wild salmon and barbecue reindeer sausage.

He wasn't as helpful as he wanted to be. In terms of mobility, passing things one-handed was the extent of his contributions. Still, he enjoyed having everyone together. In one place. Like the old days.

That too-familiar pang went through him as thoughts of his mother and sister loomed. He couldn't go there in his mind. Not now. And he couldn't think about Tally, so he made his way over to his younger brother, Aiden, walking the length of the railed gallery hallways securing fresh garland.

Pinning the pine boughs in place, Aiden looked at Marshall. Running a hand through his dark hair, he blurted out, "I'm not going back to college next semester."

That pulled Marshall's attention firmly to his brother. Marshall had busted his ass finishing college on time while staying on the rodeo circuit. "Dad's going to have a fit."

"Let him," Aiden said defiantly.

"If you don't finish college, then you don't come into your trust fund until you're twenty-five."

"I'm fully aware." He shrugged, examining the garland, securing it farther down the railing. "I'm not a child. I have a plan."

"I'm listening."

"You may have finished college, but you also found your way. I want to do the same. I'm going to work in the oil fields."

Damn. That actually sounded logical. Still, Marshall felt compelled to point out, "You're not qualified for anything more than entry level."

"Again, I'm aware. That's what I want. To prove myself."

When had his brother grown up? Marshall realized he'd viewed Aiden as perpetually a kid. Time had not frozen that day their mom and sister died. But it sure felt that way sometimes. "Okay, then. When are you going to tell Dad?"

"Soon—not tonight, but soon." Aiden looked at him sideways, gripping the railing. "I was hoping you would come with me. You have experience with not following in the old man's footsteps."

"Glad to be there for you. Whatever you need." And Marshall meant it. His eyes gravitated to Tally, and he thought about her alone for the holidays, working for others, staying in someone else's home.

What would make the occasion special for her? He found himself wanting the answer to that. To make her smile. And yes, he wanted that smile to follow a breathy sigh of pleasure when he kissed her.

Five hours later, after his family had left, he still hadn't come up with an answer. Surely inspiration could be found somewhere. Parked on the great room sofa in front of the fire, he fiddled with a pen cap, tracing its grooves. He searched the decorated space for the tendrils of a plan. Everything twinkled, but nothing seemed as fantastic as the oversize Christmas tree.

Lush boughs displayed family ornaments from his grandparents, made of spun glass, hand-painted. Precious and irreplaceable.

White lights lined the tree thanks to the joint effort of Mikkelson and Steele men. A winter wonderland. Romantic by all objective accounts. His family had gone above and beyond, and while he appreciated the effort on his behalf, he also found it brought back a few too many memories of childhood Christmases here.

Better to focus on business.

He picked up the legal pad with the brainstorming list he and his family had compiled of additional contacts for the company's marketing department, people who might be willing to donate high-priced items for the silent auction. Any pressure he could take off that whole buy-a-bachelor fund-raiser would be a bonus.

He felt the weight of Tally's eyes on him. He turned to find her holding Nugget, scratching the pup's ears. Tally's tenderness with his dog, joy riding the horse, all tugged at him with how easily she was fitting into his world.

Marshall cleared his throat, turning the legal pad upside down. "Can I help you with something?"

"Actually, I was hoping that I could help you. As I was looking around at all the family you have and seeing the decorations, it made me think of all the work holidays bring for you—along with the joy."

"What do you mean?"

Chewing her bottom lip, she took a step closer. Nugget seemed content in her arms, nuzzling closer. The dog let out a deep, relaxed sigh. "Have you finished your shopping? I thought you might appreciate some female input. You have so many people to buy for."

The light in her eyes was mesmerizing. He wasn't much for shopping. He usually just wrote checks to everyone's favorite charities. But here was his answer to how to make Christmas special for her. "Sure, we can drive into town tomorrow, look around...go out to dinner."

"Dinner, too?" She picked at her fingernails nervously. "That doesn't seem fair. I'm paid to cook for you."

"You've been working overtime, and we both know it."

"I'm trying to be professional."

He sensed her hesitation. Convincing her to go with him suddenly seemed more important than winning any rodeo. "If you weren't working for me, would you go out to dinner with me?"

"If I weren't unobtainable, would you be asking me?" she asked smartly.

He chuckled softly. "Now there's a circular argument."

She set down the dog and eased the legal pad from Marshall's hand, their fingers brushing. "Let's get started making a list of who you need to shop for so we'll know what types of stores to hit. I know of some fun, niche shops…" She paused. "Although my budget would be much different from yours. Maybe—"

"My family doesn't go overboard on Christmas gifts." Which was true enough.

"I enjoyed today." She sat beside him, her leg brushing his. A crackle of awareness snapped between them as tangibly as the *pop* of the settling log in the fire.

He wanted to reach for her, to finish this day celebrating in the best way possible. Her gaze skittered away, and she fidgeted with the pad in her hands.

The last thing he wanted was for her to feel anxious in his presence. He wanted to peel the clothes from her body and kiss every inch of her bared flesh.

However, as much as he wanted her, the timing wasn't right. "I don't want you to be nervous around me. I meant what I said about the next move being yours." He scooped up his dog and backed away. "Good night."

The flash of awareness—and yes, regret—in her eyes encouraged him. An attraction like theirs couldn't be denied. They both should let it run its course while they had the chance.

Seven

Tally had dreamed of a Christmas outing like this, the joy of sharing the simplicity of holiday shopping with someone. And the fact that the someone happened to be hot as hell in his Stetson and boots, the thick suede jacket calling to her fingers to touch, only added to the fun.

She inhaled deeply, and the scents of pine and snow filled her lungs. A sharp breath braced her, seemed to enliven her senses and anchor her to this moment. This surreal experience unfolded in the bustle of shopping. The market square hummed with holiday mayhem, couples and families milling about. An outdoor ice-skating rink was packed with people enjoying the clear weather. Under an awning, carolers in medieval costumes sang "Greensleeves."

She and Marshall had made a dent in their list in an indoor shopping mall, and now were finishing up with specialty shops. She enjoyed being outside, especially with her job calling for so much time indoors. The clean, fresh air sang through her senses.

In her gloved hand, she played with the shopping agenda—and that list of his relatives was long, so long. He'd given her some general notes for each person, helpful in choosing gifts but also in getting to know his huge family.

His sister Delaney was an ecological activist who appreciated earth-friendly "green" gifts. Many of his family had dogs as well, so pet gifts were a hit. Broderick and Glenna had a husky. His stepbrother's wife had a service dog to alert to her issues with diabetes. And his sister Naomi and her husband, Royce, had a Saint Bernard named Tessie in honor of Royce's favorite scientist, Tesla.

Buying for his father and stepmother would be a challenge, as Marshall was reticent on the subject of his father's remarriage.

He opened the door to the Little Caribou, a children's boutique store. Warm air flooded her cheeks, contrasting with the brisk December chill. She glanced down at her list. They needed to pick up a few items for Naomi's twin baby girls and Broderick's daughter. Tally wandered around the store while Marshall shopped.

An old ache in her chest, in her heart, flooded her. A life of what could have been with her baby, now nearly ten years old, enjoying Christmas. Tears pushed at the corners of her eyes, making her vision blurred. She pushed her lips together, trying to keep her emotions in check and at bay.

And Marshall's family didn't even have the comfort of knowing their lost loved ones were alive. What had she been thinking in coming here? Would learning about her father hurt them more or give them some kind of peace through answers?

She didn't know what to do.

He paused just inside the doorway, which was decorated with a wreath. "I'm sorry. I didn't mean to make you think of the sick babies in the hospital."

She felt guilty for not thinking of little Stella Rae, clinging to life in the NICU. She reached for a Baby's First Christmas ornament to hang by Stella Rae's bassinet. Tally cradled the little polar bear decoration in her palm, wishing she could somehow do more. "I know the odds when I give my heart."

"And yet you do it anyway. You're an amazing woman." He added her purchase to his growing pile. "Let me buy this."

She didn't want to take advantage. She paid her own way in the world. "But then it won't be from me."

"Wash an extra dish or dust my books again if it'll make you feel less obligated." He passed his credit card to the cashier.

She searched his face, the handsome lines, strong jaw peppered with a midday stubble. "You don't want to admit to being a good guy."

"It's a simple thing for me to do. Think what you

want about me." He passed her the red bag, white tissue paper poking out.

"I'll graciously say thank you on little Stella Rae's behalf. And on behalf of her mother, too." Her fingers tightened on the bag, the paper crackling in her grip.

"Are you okay?"

She should be asking him that question. Surely the holidays made him think of his sister. "I'm fine. Please don't worry about me."

"Are you sure? It seems like something else is on your mind."

A knot of panic started in her stomach. She wasn't sure how to broach the subject of her father, or if it was even the right thing to do.

She slipped a hand through the crook of his arm without thinking. Needing the comfort of his muscular touch. She hadn't counted on the distracting sizzle. "Let's just enjoy the day. Where should we have dinner that'll make you forget about your broken bone for a bit and get in the Christmas spirit?"

He squeezed her hand. "Kit's Kodiak Café just outside Anchorage. It's a family favorite. They serve breakfast all day."

"Sounds wonderful." She couldn't help but be entranced by the multi-millionaire with down-to-earth tastes. "I have to warn you, though, I can plow through a stack of pancakes."

"I'll keep that in mind," he said, watching her through assessing eyes as they made their way back to the SUV.

She could see in his expression he wasn't buying her "I'm fine" answer. Once in the passenger seat, she played with her seat belt, a plan forming. An urgency overtaking her as he drove his SUV to the café. Tally swallowed once, determination settling inside her. She would tell him about her child. If he judged her for it, then she was better off knowing now. It would make keeping her distance all the easier.

Well, not easier, but simpler, at least. And then he would stop asking her what was on her mind.

She stared out the window, the sun already setting in the short Alaskan day, Christmas lights winking to life through the town. "You asked me why I rock the babies."

"Your charitable spirit. Yes, I remember."

"My reasons really are more about me…" She picked at the hem of her puffy parka. "About my past."

He shot her a quick glance, his grip firm on the wheel. "What do you mean?"

She drew in a shaky breath. "When I was nineteen, I had a baby that I gave up for adoption."

He stayed silent for a moment, a slight lift of his eyebrows the only sign he'd registered her words. Then he slipped his arm from the sling and rested his hand on her knee. "That had to be a difficult decision to make."

"I knew it was the right thing." She welcomed the comfort of his touch. There'd been so little to carry her through those first days. And while she was at peace with her choice, it still hurt. "Actually, following through on the decision? That was the rough part. More than I can put into words."

"I'm so sorry." He squeezed her knee, his hand warm through her denim.

Even knowing she owed no one an explanation, she couldn't stem the impulse to explain to him. "I was alone, no money, the baby's father wanted nothing to do with me or our child." That betrayal cut so deep even now. She knew now she'd only chosen to be with him to fill a void after her father's suicide, but still, being let down so horribly by someone she'd thought she loved cut to the core.

She drew in a bracing breath and plowed forward. "I got to meet the couple before the adoption. They'd gone through multiple fertility treatments, and even carried one baby to the seventh month only to have their premature newborn pass away three weeks later."

He stayed silent, listening. She liked that about him, the way he didn't feel the need to fill the air with platitudes. This was so much more complicated. "The mom told me about how she and her husband had taken turns staying at the NICU with their child. And then one afternoon they both left for the cafeteria to have lunch together. Their baby died while they were away. Intellectually, she knew they weren't responsible. But she said she just wished someone had been holding her little one…"

"So that's why you rock premature babies," he said with unerring insight.

"It's my way of giving back to the couple who are loving parents to my son." She pressed her hand to his. "Don't say anything."

He lifted her hand and pressed a kiss to her palm, then clasped it, giving her more of that comfort and beautiful silent acceptance.

This man was so much more than a rodeo hunk or wealthy rancher. He was a caring man. And that posed a greater risk than any physical temptation.

She needed to get her focus back on the job and off her boss.

Leather steering wheel gliding between his palms, Marshall maneuvered the SUV in the dark streets. He hung a left, the vehicle smooth as a hot knife through butter as he guided it toward home. On the edge of the horizon, a touch of northern lights painted the sky with greens and yellows in growing brilliance. He looked forward to watching them with Tally. Their dinner together had passed in a flash of easy conversation.

She hadn't been kidding. She'd put down a stack of pancakes along with reindeer sausage. She'd been social and charming, but there was a definite distance between them. Maybe she regretted sharing about the baby she'd given up for adoption. He wasn't sure, and he could sense this wasn't the time to push her about being together. She reminded him of a skittish horse: one wrong move and she would bolt.

Right now, she was all business, her phone out as

she typed in her to-do list for the fund-raiser, focusing on the menu. She'd been quizzing him on family food preferences and allergies—as if he knew that.

She tapped on the screen, the glow reflecting up to highlight hints of gold in her auburn hair. "I'll be making a spreadsheet of all the items needed for the menu—"

"We have caterers," he reminded her.

"For some things, sure. Like for the gala. But for Christmas... I'm here for a reason. I want to make sure there are no wasted ingredients."

"You could donate unused items."

"Hmm..." She tapped her phone to her chin, drawing his attention to her lovely face. "Once something's opened, then all of it should be used."

He leveled a glance at her. "I'm not sure what they're paying you, but I suspect it's not nearly enough."

Her smile went wider, her face illuminated by the dash lights. "I do believe there's a compliment in there. Thank you."

He wanted to compliment her on more than her professionalism, but she'd only just started to relax again. So he offered a more general explanation. "I don't want you to overwork yourself. I'll ask my family what things they might want to make over the holidays. Traditional stuff."

The whole blended Christmas thing would be a challenge. Merging traditions never seemed to be without hiccups.

"Hmm." She wagged a finger at him. "Very slick

of you to figure out a way for me not to stuff your turkey with sprouts."

God, he liked the way she made him laugh. Holidays were usually hell for him, and somehow, she was making this one more than bearable. Fun even.

"All right, now," she said, directing her attention back to her phone, red hair pooling in front of her, making her seem mysterious, like a siren from a classic film. "Moving along to the drink menu. What kind of beer and wine do you prefer?"

Her words iced the warmth between them. He turned his focus back to the road. "You choose. The party scene isn't for me."

"This is just a fund-raiser thrown by your family's business—at Christmastime, no less." She held her hands in front of the blasting heater. "I hardly think that qualifies as barhopping."

"I keep a tight rein on my life." He had to. It could spiral out of control with just one slip.

"What do you mean?" Her voice was laced with deep, genuine concern.

He weighed his words. "I know myself and what I want for my future."

"What would that be?"

"Peace."

"I think there are many people who feel that way." She toyed with her cell phone. "I guess it's none of my business, really. I'm sorry to be nosy."

For a reason he couldn't decipher, he found himself admitting, "I'm a recovering alcoholic."

The words settled between them. For a moment,

a half a heartbeat that felt a helluva lot longer, he wondered if such an admission had been wise. But Marshall heard her draw in a sympathetic breath.

She set aside her cell phone carefully, directing her full attention to him. "I didn't know."

"No one does, other than my support group." He turned at a corner, the new Christmas flags on streetlamps flapping in the snowy wind.

"Why are you telling me, then?"

He searched for an explanation that made some kind of sense. "I had a particularly intense meeting with my sponsor. Keeping this locked in—faking everyone out by drinking nonalcoholic beer and water in drink glasses—isn't a healthy way to live." He glanced at her to gauge her reaction. "I guess I'm trying out the openness on you first since you were so open with me about your past."

She looked away, fidgeting with her phone. "How long have you been sober?"

"Just over four years." Four years. Two months. Seventeen days.

"You said you had an intense meeting with your sponsor recently?"

"Every day is a battle." He didn't see the need to go into detail about how wanting her, envisioning her in his life, was adding to the tension every day. "Holidays are tough. And parties are the worst with all the alcohol flowing. It causes talk if I don't drink, so there are times I hold a drink or bottle and fake it just to keep the questions from driving me crazy."

She stroked her thumb across the screen to her

phone, where she'd been making her list. "I can see why opening up from the get-go might make things easier."

"Maybe." His sponsor had said the same, but even testing that out with Tally was tougher than he expected. He pushed himself ahead, eyes fixed on the growing strength of the northern lights. He found them anchoring. "You're probably wondering what my story is."

"Of course I'm wondering, but it's up to you if you want to tell me." Her voice was soft, caressing the air between them with understanding.

"You're good at the passive-aggressive technique." He steered the SUV through the main gate leading to his property, onto the winding road to his home. Thick trees reached toward the sky, providing him with a sense of security. There were worse settings for a heart-to-heart than on his land, his space.

"I'm not so sure that's a compliment."

"I started on the rodeo circuit young and partied hard, too hard. Before I knew it, I needed the drinks to function." Now that he'd started speaking, the words flowed from him like bourbon from a bottle, smooth and biting all at once. "Then I found out what a beast booze can be. It seduces you, then turns on you and you're so far underperforming you're ready to crash and burn." The vehicle jostled along the icy road, the ranch looming ahead. Home.

"That's what happened to you? A crash?"

He stopped at the side entrance, shifting the SUV into Park, idling. He killed the headlights so that the only light in the vehicle came from the motion sensors outside the garage. After a minute, they'd flick off, too.

"I took a fall so bad in the ring it landed me in the hospital." He rubbed his cast lightly, leaning back in his seat. "After that, I checked myself into rehab and pulled back from the circuit. I only do charity functions now."

"I imagine the broken arm brought back some painful memories," she said insightfully.

God, she was easy to talk to. "This didn't even happen in the ring. It was a simple accident afterward. I was thinking too much about the past and got distracted."

"I'm so sorry." She stroked along his cast. "But I'm also glad it wasn't worse."

"That's one way to look at it."

She tipped her head, catching his eyes. "What would you have said to someone in your group who shared what you just did? I assume you're in Alcoholics Anonymous since you said you have a sponsor."

A solid question. He thought through to the obvious answer he should have come to on his own. "I would remind them to attend meetings—which I do. You're a good person with good instincts."

"It's more than instinct." Her face pinched with pain. She pushed back her wavy hair with a shaky hand. "It's experience. My father struggled with inner demons of his own. Sometimes he drank too much to quiet those demons."

"I'm sorry." He understood well from confidences at meetings how much grief alcoholism could bring to relatives, part of why he'd tried so hard to keep his problems from his family.

A part of why he'd stayed alone on the ranch?

He shuffled aside the distracting thought and focused on Tally.

"My mother and I begged him to get help, but he was resistant." She looked at him quickly, then averted her eyes. "He wasn't physically abusive, so he insisted he didn't have a problem. He just couldn't accept the other ways it affected his life."

He could hear the lack of peace in her soft tone, the burden of it still hanging over her. "And now your parents are gone. I'm so very sorry."

"It's tough to know there's no do-over to make things right," she said, her voice cracking.

He shifted in his seat, reaching out his good arm and stroking her fragile shoulder. Her hair glided across his wrist in a silken wave. "You're living your life to the fullest. I'm sure they would be proud."

"I hope so."

Such sadness radiated from her he ached to pull her into his arms, to take on all that hurt for her. But he couldn't forget his promise to leave any move up to her. So he simply caressed her shoulder, his fingers sketching lightly along her back.

Even with his determination to keep his distance unless she made a move, his senses went on high alert, fine-tuning into the moment—the hum of the idling engine, the whisper of the heater. Northern lights streaked through the sky, casting a multicolored hue through the vehicle's cab, giving her a luminescent glow.

Heat pumped through him until he went hard with want. The spark of awareness in her eyes intensified, echoing in him.

She swayed closer. Closer again. All the encouragement he needed. He angled nearer, sealing his mouth to hers. The connection was instantaneous and combustible. Her palms slid over his chest, gripping his jacket with urgency. Her lips parted, welcoming him.

An invitation he couldn't resist.

He swept his tongue over hers, exploring, the taste of syrup and her an enticing blend that called to him to take more. As much as she would give.

Her hands slid around his neck, her fingers threading through his hair. Desire pumped through him, urging him on for more. Grateful his arm was free of the sling, he pressed her back against the seat, her chest to his, the softness of her breasts searing him even through their jackets. He burned to get rid of their clothes, to sample every inch of her creamy skin.

Her kittenish sighs encouraged him, the chemistry deepened by the day they'd shared, the ways they'd bared their secrets to each other. He wanted more. All of her, craving her so much that he couldn't trust himself.

As he eased back to suggest they take things inside, he saw the wariness in her eyes; the full weight of their conversation hit him. Her father had been an alcoholic. That had left a painful mark on her she wouldn't want to repeat in her personal life.

Which left him firmly on the outside.

Eight

Felicity tugged on her ponytail, shouldering open the snowflake-plastered door leading into the cafeteria. Bright fluorescents shone down unforgiving white light on the circular blue tables. Her flats slipped slightly, the tread on the sole of her shoes worn from constant movement.

Stabilizing herself, she moved toward the table in the far corner where Conrad, handsome as always, sat in a sharp gray business suit, a buff Stetson on the chair beside him.

For the fourth time this week giving up part of his workday to drive across town for her.

A fact she wasn't mad about at all. Actually, butterflies stirred in her stomach over how quickly this was starting to feel like a normal routine. As if they'd been meeting on her lunch breaks for years.

Felicity had worried over the first meeting. Assumed the silver fox would attempt to win her through pressure. She'd been pleasantly surprised at his laid-back demeanor.

She wasn't sure how much longer he would continue this before making his big move, but she had to admit she was curious. He could woo her with expensive outings and gifts, but he gave his time instead. And to her, that was a much more precious commodity. Although she might never know how long he would keep this up, as her client here at the hospital was due to be discharged within a week. She would return to regular case duty.

She should be rejoicing for her little client's health, but she would miss these lunches. She liked him, but knew this couldn't go anywhere. She had her career on track, had even applied for a social worker's job at the hospital. Her dream position. Her divorce had left her so gutted, her career had gone off the rails.

She wouldn't lose all she'd regained.

Felicity wove past a table full of staff, toward the handsome man who'd not only reserved a table for her but also had bought their meal—he'd texted her earlier for her order. Conrad's smile was as bright as the string of white Christmas lights that framed the kitchen door behind him.

"Hello." She slung her leather bag on the spare

seat as he pulled out her chair for her. "I'm not sure how this has become a habit so quickly."

"In business, I'm known as a persuasive, persistent man. How was your day?" He handed her a steaming cup of soy vanilla chai latte. Her favorite midday pick-me-up from the coffee- and teahouse just up the street. Accepting it from his outstretched hand, her fingers brushed his ever so slightly.

Felicity did her best to bury the tug of a smile, inhaling the spice of clove and vanilla from the steam. Christmas in a cup.

Her client was doing well, but Tally's little charge was in critical condition. It could be so heartbreaking in the NICU. "Busy. But I don't want to talk about that." Felicity wanted to learn more about what made this man tick. What made him willing to eat crummy cafeteria food day after day? Was he just about the chase? "Tell me about your family's plans for the fund-raiser."

Those piercing eyes turned thoughtful. There was something earnest in his chiseled jaw. "Tally has been a godsend in getting things organized out at the ranch. Marshall was resistant, but she's really helped bring him around." He stuck a straw in his tea. "We've all been worried about him since he broke his arm. He works himself into the ground managing the ranch, but he lives for it. Being out of commission has been difficult for an active guy like him."

A family shuffled by with a man in a green hospital gown. She couldn't miss the fatigue in his eyes as he wheezed, trying his best to sing "Jingle Bells" with two little girls about six years old. Small attempts at the Christmas spirit even in this blinding room touched her heart. As they took their seats at the table by the Christmas tree, she saw something like resilience in the way the man sat in his chair, smiling at the pretty blonde next to him.

She couldn't help but be moved, wondering if her own outlook on life was too pessimistic, ironic given that she counseled others.

"I'm glad things are working out. She's happy to have this job opportunity." Tally had been pleased at how accommodating her boss was about her volunteer schedule. The interest in her eyes was impossible to miss, as was the wariness. Felicity didn't know the reason for it, but she worried for her friend.

"Jack and Jeannie are pleased with the progress. It'll make quite a splash for the start of their charitable foundation to honor their spouses who died." Conrad shoveled three fries into his mouth.

"They're lucky to have found love twice in a lifetime. Most don't find that kind of connection even once." She dug into her burger.

"While I have my reservations about all this blending of families with our former business rival, I'm grateful Jack has Jeannie for support right now." He swiped his mouth with a napkin. "I don't know how much you've heard, but this merger hasn't been as smooth as we like to make out. There are leaks."

"There always are." She let out a deep sigh, aware

of how difficult things could be from the ugly power of privileged information made public.

"True enough. And people out to extort or hurt the family." His face went tight. "Like the nut-job who wrangled her way into the company, then claimed my niece didn't die in the crash. It's insane and impossible, but still hurt my brother like hell."

"And you, too," she said softly.

He nodded once, then set his burger aside. "The woman—she calls herself Milla Jones—cut and ran into Canada. But we'll find her and get to the bottom of her agenda."

The phrasing caught Felicity off guard, and she choked on a bite of burger. Pressing her hand to her mouth, she coughed before finding the words on her tongue. "'Calls herself'?"

"Yeah," he said, his face taking on an all-business, all-facts air, but she could sense the tension underlying it. "We have investigators looking for her. They've managed to locate a DNA sample off a brush she used at the office. With luck, there will be a hit in the system that gives us more information."

"This has to be so hard on your family." She could see the toll it was taking on him, and her heart tugged. "Your brother's lucky to have your support." She'd done her own research and knew Conrad pinch-hit for his brother personally and professionally, even though Conrad had a full life of his own running his investments corporation. She also saw from her search that he didn't have any children of his own. "You're close to your nieces and nephews."

"They're like surrogate kids, I guess." He swiped a fat fry through ketchup. "I haven't had much luck building that family of my own. Got divorced before making it to our first anniversary. Then another engagement fell apart just shy of the altar."

"I'm so sorry."

For a moment, Conrad seemed distant. As if he replayed the broken relationships before his eyes on some phantom screen. But only for a beat. Shoulders shrugging, he looked at her. "It's in the past."

"Divorce is hell." She knew that all too well. Her ex had cheated, blown through her small inheritance, then dragged the divorce out in court for heaven only knew what reason other than to torture and potentially bankrupt them both.

"Ah, I'm sorry yours was painful."

She didn't bother denying what he could no doubt see on her face. "I won't go through it again. Under any circumstances. Do you understand what I'm saying?"

He gave her a lopsided grin, his enticing cowboy charm shining. "I don't recall proposing."

"You sure did put me in my place."

"Stop thinking so much, and let's just enjoy being together." He bit into his burger, chewing thoughtfully while watching her. "I hope you'll be attending the fund-raiser. I've already purchased a ticket for you."

And there it was. The push for more, even if it

was just chemistry. And she found she wanted to throw caution to the wind and go with him.

Tally shut off her car and let her head fall to rest on her steering wheel. Tears she'd held in check for the drive flooded free. She'd volunteered for a couple of years, and this never got easier. Little Stella Rae was in critical condition, and Tally's heart was tearing in two.

A tap on her window pulled her upright. She swept aside her tears and found Marshall standing in the snow. She rolled down the window. "I'll be there in a minute."

He leaned an arm on the open window, blocking the wind with his broad shoulders. "What's wrong?"

"I'm fine." She forced a smile, gathering her purse. "I just want to get to work."

"Forget it, really." He opened the door and offered his hand. "Dishes don't matter. You matter. Let me make you something to eat and you can unload—if you want to talk. If not, we'll just share a meal. I've got some caribou stew I can defrost."

What he offered sounded nothing short of amazing, sharing her burden with someone at the end of the day. She'd been alone for so long. Nodding, she stepped from the car. "Thank you."

The dampness freezing on her cheeks and reminding her of her fears for the little girl, Tally followed Marshall into the house, to the kitchen.

He waved away her offer of help, and she sagged to sit at the table. "I should be used to this by now."

"Used to what?" he asked, putting the container into the microwave and tapping Defrost.

"The baby I've been rocking at the hospital took a turn for the worse. The doctors don't know if she'll make it through the night." The words tumbled free, threatening a fresh wash of tears.

He straightened from the counter. "Do you want me to drive you back up to the hospital?"

"Her mother's with her. They need time alone together…in case…" She couldn't hold back the tears any longer, sobs overtaking her.

Marshall knelt beside her, sliding an arm around her shoulders. Her head fell to rest against his chest—she couldn't resist—and she let herself take the comfort he offered. His strong touch and the warm flannel of his shirt against her cheek seeped through her senses. He didn't try to cheer her. He simply held her and waited.

She sniffled against his chest, her breath steadying, although her heart began to pick up pace. "I'm sorry I can't tell you more, but I'm not allowed to talk about patients at the hospital in any detail, not even as a volunteer."

"I understand. I'm here for whatever you need." His hand circled her back.

"Thank you. It means a lot to me." All her pent-up emotion began to shift, to gather force seeking an outlet of another kind. Butterflies stirred in her stomach, her skin tingling.

"It must be difficult not talking about what you

go through volunteering." His breath was warm against her hair.

"Volunteering with Felicity helps," she answered, her fingers playing lightly along his chest, "but yes, it's not the same as being able to let it all out. I knew the rules, though, when I signed on…" Her words trailed off, and unable to stop herself, she tipped her face to his and kissed him.

His lips were hot and mobile on hers. Pressing. Sliding. Parting. He groaned against her mouth, his lips sealing to hers. An explosion of want showered through her at the feel of his tongue tracing along hers. All the restrained attraction hitting her when she was too vulnerable to resist. Too many emotions bombarded her, but in him she found the perfect outlet.

She slid her arms around his neck, drawing him closer. Wanting more. Needing more.

Needing him.

Her breasts ached, and she craved the feel of him against her. She inched closer. Closer still. She stood and he followed suit, their legs tangling as he pressed her against the wall, the contact only making her hunger for more. He slipped free from his sling, his body fitting to hers, setting her senses on fire. She burned for him. She trailed her hands down his back, digging into his hips and bringing him closer.

He eased his mouth from hers, his forehead against hers as he swept Tally's hair from her face with broad, urgent hands. "Tally, no, not now."

"Yes, now." Her fingers gripped his shirt urgently.

She was breathless with need. "You told me I only had to make the first move and you would follow through."

"This isn't the same. You're too upset to think clearly. I can't take advantage of that."

"I want you." She willed him to hear the truth in her voice. "I'm an adult capable of making my own decisions."

"As am I. And I'm not going to have you regret this in the morning." His words rang with a deep resolution.

And nobility.

Damn. He was a good man. And maybe he had a point. Even if it hurt right now to acknowledge as much.

Perhaps there was a middle ground. Her breath left her in a shaky sigh. "What if we sleep together tonight, and if I feel the same way when I wake in your arms in the morning…"

"Then I'll take great pleasure in saying yes." He looped an arm under her bottom and lifted her. "I'll bring dinner up for us later. For now, we'll just enjoy the moment."

Delicious anticipation filled her as she realized his intent. She hooked her arms around his neck and wrapped her legs around his waist. A husky growl of appreciation rumbled in his chest. He secured his hold and began winding his way through the hall and up the stairs to his master suite.

Pausing in the doorway, he kissed her again in that soul-melting way of his. As he leaned against the doorjamb, she caressed his beard-stubbled face, tracing the now-familiar strength of his jaw. With a low moan, he lifted his mouth from hers, securing his hold on her again as he straightened from the doorway.

A fireplace crackled, beckoning her across the hardwood floor, drawing her attention to the far wall where floor-to-ceiling windows let snippets of moonglow in. The room, dusky in the yellow firelight, was as large as her apartment. Above the mantel, an oversize painting showed a herd of horses galloping across a valley. A stuffed gray chair faced the fire, with a thick book sitting on top of a white blanket.

Simple. Modest. But not bare. Between the deep kiss at the threshold and his sure footsteps toward the bed, she felt her heart race. Hands touching his always-tousled black hair. Appreciating the softness of his locks as she felt the power of his muscles holding her up.

He lowered her to the plush white rug by the bed, sweeping back the spread. They stepped out of their shoes, leaving them side by side. He guided her to lay down beside him and covered them both.

Pressing against him felt so good. As much as she wanted to have sex with him tonight, she also knew she was in no state to think straight. His restraint, his nobility, meant so much.

She rested her head on his shoulder. "Tell me about when you were a child."

Shifting, she sank deeper into the mattress, into

him. She folded into his body, curving around his chest, legs tangling together. His fingers moved down her back, and she could feel the tight strength of his muscles in the way his arm flexed.

A sigh rippled through her, and she breathed in his musky scent. Wishing she could suspend this moment in time forever. Let this time play for infinity. The feel of the sheets against her skin. His strong touch.

"My maternal grandmother used to tell us local legends as bedtime stories. But Mother found inventive ways to keep us in touch with our Alaskan Native heritage." His deep voice was a rumble in his chest and hers, too.

Her fingers stroked over his flannel shirt, the cotton fabric and pearl buttons warm from his body. The button fly of his jeans pressed to her hip, the steely length of him letting her know what this restraint cost him.

Her hands tunneled beneath his flannel shirt and found their way to his skin, striking his chest. "How so?"

"Have you heard of an ulu?" He traced small circles down her back.

"It's a kind of hunting knife, right?"

"Yes, used for seal and walrus skinning."

"I'm not sure this bedtime story is sounding very peaceful."

He chuckled lightly. "My mother used the knife as a pizza cutter—no seals or walrus were harmed at her hand."

A soft laugh in response filled the raw spaces inside her. "That's priceless."

"She was an incredible mom."

She caressed his jaw, fingers appreciating every angle. "I'm so sorry you lost your mother."

"I'm sorry you lost yours." He pressed a kiss to her palm, his stubble a sweet abrasion against her skin. "Thank you for listening to me talk about her. How about I get us both some supper now and bring it back up here? Then I would like to hear about yours."

"I would like that," she said, settling back into the pillow and watching him walk across the room, his broad shoulders and long legs a feast for her eyes. The flex of his muscles as he moved spoke of hard work and strength. He'd ditched his sling and held his cast arm against his chest. He moved like a caged animal, desperate to spring into action. Her heart stung over the frustration he must feel.

He was getting harder to resist on so many levels, like in how easily they'd talked. Already she thought about telling him of her mom, and the fairy-tale collectable ornaments they'd picked out each Christmas. Her dad had usually been on a bender, holidays particularly bad for his drinking. The ornaments had gotten lost when her father died, and sorting through even their meager belongings had been so very difficult. She only had the mermaid ornament left, the one she kept as a charm on her key chain. But if she told Marshall about her mom, then it would inevitably lead to talking about her dad. And she selfishly wanted to hold on to this connection with Marshall for a while longer.

Yes, she and Marshall both knew life wasn't always fair. But for tonight, here, it felt more incredible than she could remember.

Marshall's dreams had been filled with images of making love to Tally since the day she'd arrived. Of his mouth on her. Her lips on him. He pushed aside his concerns about being with her, because, damn it, he wanted her. Even more now that they'd been together in what was the most incredible night he'd ever experienced.

His body was coming alive hard and fast with the realization she was kissing him awake. He tunneled his hands through the covers to find her, the room still dimly illuminated by moonlight streaming through the windows and flames flickering in the fireplace. His internal clock told him it wasn't quite morning yet, but they'd both slept.

And then his brain went on stun with the sweet wriggle of her body against his. "Tally…"

She nipped his bottom lip, her leg between his, her thigh pressing against his erection. "You said if I still wanted you in the morning that you would be happy to comply."

"I did." And while he hadn't expected her to still take him up on it, he was damn glad she had.

"Well, it's morning. Or close enough." She writhed against him with unmistakable intent. "And I still want you. So very much."

Her words fired through him, stoking his ever-present desire for her.

He cradled her bottom in his hands and wished the damn cast was off. "I've wanted this since the first time I laid eyes on you."

"That can't be so." She kissed along his ear, her voice husky. "You told me to leave."

He rolled her to her back, pinning her with his body and his gaze. "I said I didn't need a house-keeper. That's totally different."

Her eyebrows pinched together for a moment. "So you let me stay because you were hoping to get me into your bed?"

She stroked along his calf with her toes, the movement allowing his hips to sink deeper into hers. Driving him higher. Making him crazy for her.

"Actually—" he braced with his good arm, skimming his mouth down her neck, along the collar of her flowing long T-shirt "—I was hoping you would leave so I could pursue you with a clear conscience." Or at least that's what he realized now.

"And yet here we are." She slid her hands inside the waistband of his jeans, her fingers digging into his hips.

The vision of her auburn hair splayed across his pillow sent a possessive surge through him, along with a determination to sear himself as firmly in her mind as she was in his. "We have entirely too many clothes on."

"I agree." She made fast work of the buttons on

his flannel shirt, wrestling it down over his cast, then tossing it aside.

"Slow down. My turn," he said, pressing her back into the pillow. She smiled her smoky consent.

Inching down her body, he peeled off her leggings, kissing a path along her stomach, over her hip, then down one leg while he stroked the other with his fingertips. She moaned encouragement that stirred him hotter. Harder.

Her milky skin gleamed, bathed in the glow of the moonlight and fire, and he couldn't get enough of looking at her. He tossed aside her leggings, her green lace panties peeking from the hem of her tee. Suddenly desperate to know if her bra matched, he swept aside her cotton shirt and…

Yes.

Emerald green lace cupped the sweet curves of her breasts. And as much as he savored seeing her, he wanted to see more.

Smiling, she clasped his wrists, stopping him. She eased her hands back and reached behind her to unhook the scrap of lace. The straps slipped forward, the cups catching on the curves of her breasts. His heart hammered in his chest for a half dozen heartbeats until her bra slid free.

His breath hitched in his throat. The sheer beauty of her stole the air from his lungs. He leaned forward to capture a pert peak in his mouth, teasing and loving her to a pebbling hardness. Her fingers threaded through his hair as she guided him, her head falling back.

"Protection?" she asked in husky desperation.

"Yes, I'll be right back." He pressed a lingering kiss to her before easing off the bed and walking to the bathroom. He reached into the medicine cabinet for a box of condoms and returned to the bedroom. He ditched his jeans before climbing back into bed with her.

Reclined on the pillow, she extended a hand for him. She linked fingers with him, then pulled him down to her.

His cast...damn it...

"I've got this," she said, intuitively pressing against his shoulders until he lay on his back. She straddled his hips, a sexy vision over him.

She stroked the length of his erection, cupping and cradling him, driving him to the edge before easing back. She rolled the condom down the length of him, her gaze holding his until he couldn't keep his eyes open any longer. Her touch threatened to send him over the edge.

Then she guided him inside her, slowly, deeply. He wished he had both hands available, but he intended to make full use of his free one to caress her, one breast, then the other, taking pleasure in watching the blush of pleasure pinken her flesh.

Their bodies moved together, finding a rhythm and fit unique to their mating. The blankets pooled around her waist, the cool winter air brushing over his heated flesh. Her hips rolled as he thrust, again and again, her breathy sighs filling his ears with encouragement. She scored her fingernails lightly along his chest, a trickle of perspiration between her breasts.

The image of her over him would be seared in his mind forever, the beauty of her face as she neared her completion. Her hair tumbled over her shoulders in a red cloud. She was fire and light. And even though he was on the brink of a mind-blowing orgasm, he hadn't begun to slake his craving for her.

He slid his hand between them, seeking and finding the tight bundle of nerves between her legs. She arched closer, her hips rolling against him. Her breath hitched faster and faster.

Desire pulsed through him, hot and thick in his veins. He burned to finish, but held back, needing to see her come first. Determined for her to find as much pleasure as she brought him.

The warmth of her clamped around him as her orgasm took her. She cried out, her back bowing before she folded forward to rest on his chest.

He thrust once, twice, his own pleasure racking through him hard, more intense than anything he'd experienced before. She was all he'd fantasized about and more. He slung his arm around her, holding her close as wave after wave crashed through him.

Her heart hammered against his own, which still raced in the aftermath. Their bodies sealed, flesh to flesh, he buried his hand in her hair. He'd known their chemistry would be explosive, but he couldn't have possibly anticipated this instantaneous connection their first time together.

And already, he knew this wouldn't be their last.

Nine

Tally wasn't sure how long this could last with Marshall, but she was determined to make the most of it while she could. Her secrets would have to come out soon. She owed that to him. She hadn't come here for this…and yet here she was. Indulging in the best sex of her life.

Sleeping in against his chest had been incredible, then making love, a combination she'd never expected to experience. Both passion and peace.

Waking up the second time to a text from baby Stella Rae's mother that the infant had made it through the night and taken a decided turn for the better had sent Tally's spirit soaring. Marshall had suggested they celebrate in the hot tub connected to the enclosed pool.

An enticing invitation too perfect to resist.

As she straddled his lap, the waters swirling around them, she lost herself in the rippling sensations of her fading orgasm. Marshall reclined back, his cast arm in a plastic sleeve he used for showering. His other arm banded around her, his hand stroking along her spine.

Thinking of the first day she'd seen him boldly—recklessly—in the pool to save his dog brought a smile to her face. She'd been deeply drawn to him that day, but she couldn't have dreamed they would end up like this.

Her chest against his, her breasts tingled in the aftermath. She couldn't take her hands off him, the wide expanse of his shoulders, his broad back, all of him.

Nugget curled up tight on the brown lounger. Mellow and content. A feeling Tally, too, understood. Felt take root in her chest. Even if somewhere in the back of her mind, the idea of living on borrowed time loomed. But she would not give that part of her mind any more attention. At least not now.

No. She anchored herself to the present. To the scent of musk and man. The feel of those soft lips, that strong back.

Tally pressed words onto his skin, hoping his body could soak up her gratitude. Her appreciation. "Thank you for being there for me last night."

"My pleasure." His voice rumbled in his chest against hers.

She laughed softly. "More than that. Thank you

for understanding how upset I was. I wish I could
have explained more, but when I volunteer at the
hospital, I've agreed not to share details about the
patients."

"I understand about confidentiality." He hesitated, his chin resting against her head. "It's a core
tenet of Alcoholics Anonymous."

Her breath caught in her throat as everything
went still inside her. She wasn't sure what to say
and didn't want to stop him from sharing what was
on his mind by saying the wrong thing. But the news
that he was an alcoholic had rocked her the night
he'd confided the truth. His admission had touched
her because of the level of trust he'd shown her. But
the knowledge that he suffered that way for the accident her father caused only made the deep river
of guilt inside her threaten to overflow.

His hand continued to move along her back in
rhythmic sweeps. "I need you to understand what
it means to be an alcoholic."

"I'm listening." She kept her head against his
shoulder, the waters swirling around them, leaving
droplets on his skin.

"I've been dry for four years. But an alcoholic can
never consider himself cured." His arm twitched,
holding her tighter. "I can attest to the fact that every
day is a battle to stay sober."

Once, she'd read if one violin was struck, the
chord could be felt on another violin. A connection.
An awakening. She'd never seen such a thing for her-

self, but believed in the image. Tally had that feeling right now—a shared reverberation as he spoke.

"It's admirable that you've turned your life around." Her father hadn't been able to conquer his demons, and it cost him his life. How different might her world have been if he'd found his way to getting help? To turning his life around?

"I attend Alcoholics Anonymous meetings regularly. I have a sponsor. They deserve the credit."

She angled back to look him in the eyes. "You made the step to join and stick with it. That speaks volumes."

His jaw went tight, and he shook his head. He hooked his arm around her waist and shifted her to the side, his cast arm resting along the back behind her shoulders. Their legs pressed against each other underwater.

She waited, letting him find his pace to share.

"I can't take credit. I wouldn't have even gone to AA if it had just been me in that hospital after my accident. It was my life to throw away," he said, his voice gravelly. "But I didn't tell you that in that accident I was drunk. I'd ridden drunk before—but I always told myself it was my life. But that time I was thrown, and the horse trampled one of the guys hauling my ass out of there. It landed us both in the hospital."

"That had to have been so terrifying." Just thinking about it made her stomach lurch.

"It was. He could have been killed."

"You could have died, too." A flicker of unease

went through her as she thought of her father's death wish. Had Marshall battled those same thoughts? Did he wrestle with that element still?

He cricked his neck from side to side. "After that, I retired from the circuit and got myself clean. I make guest appearances for charity, but there's no way I can go back to the lifestyle."

She shook her head, unwilling to let him blame himself for his arm. "But it was an accident. Accidents can happen to anyone."

"Nuh-uh… It was avoidable. I was distracted."

She narrowed her eyes, swiping aside damp hair clinging to the sides of her face. "By what?"

His ragged breath brushed her bare skin. "Thinking about my mom and sister who died."

She flinched, in pain for him, and also as she was reminded again of her father and the secret she needed to share with Marshall. But now didn't seem the right time. "I'm so sorry."

"I should know that kind of distraction can happen at any time. It's a big part of what drove me to the rodeo circuit. I was running from my family and reminders of what it used to be like."

Guilt pierced her over her father's role in that pain, such crushing loss. She'd come here wanting to make amends, but now she realized that telling this family would also be a burden to them, dredging up the past at a time when they were already so raw because of the mysterious woman's claim that Breanna was still alive.

The secret about her father would have to be told

eventually; there was no avoiding that. But the fallout would be so much worse than she'd anticipated. Choosing the right time to tell Marshall weighed on her. Heavily.

Tally shivered in spite of the heated waters caressing her body. She'd come here for peace and to move forward with her life. And, instead, found herself stuck even deeper in the past.

Marshall slid his SUV into Park outside his father's home, finding himself needing to alert his father to a tough decision—that he planned to go public about his alcoholism, an important step in moving forward with his life.

The past couple of weeks with Tally had been incredible. It had been difficult for him to focus on work, instead drawn to spending as much time with her as possible—dinners out, walks in the snow, evenings making love by the fire. The more time he spent with her, the more he wanted. All the reasons it wasn't wise grew harder to remember.

The icy water reflected the redwood mansion. The bay stretched with ice and hints of blue, deep as the sky above. Hard to believe life could get so complicated with views like this.

Yet here Marshall was, leading a very complicated life despite the simple beauty of this land.

He pressed the lock button on his SUV. Birds in the tall pine tree nearby took off as the beep resounded through the Steele family compound. His boots crunched through the snow toward the barn where his father had texted him to meet him.

With the expanded family, the barn on the grounds had been under what felt like constant renovation. More stalls were needed for more horses. He studied the newest section of the structure, aware of every change, from the higher ceilings and automatic feeders to the new flooring and drainage systems that kept the place clean. More evidence that business as usual meant massive change and restructuring. No doubt his father had adapted well—professionally and personally—after the way the Steele family had been emotionally devastated. More power to the old man.

Marshall thought about upgrading the old barn at his place and using it to expand the ranch, taking on more staff. Thanks to the success of his investments, he had the financial flexibility to grow the riding school and the stud farm. He wondered why he hadn't considered it before.

Jack Steele lifted an orange bucket of feed at the back of the barn. His puffy jacket brushed against the stall door. His father's dark hair appeared darker in the muted light of the barn. The electric lights above had yet to be wired. Willow, a paint horse, chewed lazily on a piece of hay as Marshall approached.

Wearing a black Stetson, Jack nodded in greeting. "Hello, son. Good to see you. What brings you over this way?"

Marshall's eyes widened. How could his dad say

everything and yet nothing? Hands in the pockets of his jeans, Marshall shook his head. He searched for the right words to share what was on his mind, and then realized how he always found his way best. "I thought we could go for a ride. Maybe I could try out the new mustang. Flash, right?"

Jack shot a pointed glance toward Marshall's cast. "What about your arm?"

A wad of frustration filled his chest. He knew what he needed to do to alleviate the pressure. He adjusted his own Stetson, shaking his head. "I'm going stir-crazy staying off a horse. I've ridden one-handed in the ring on horses trying to toss me on my ass. I think I can handle staying in the saddle with a regular ride."

"Fair enough. I understand how it feels to be an unwilling patient."

Jack had suffered a critical riding accident earlier in the year, breaking his C1 and C2 vertebrae. It was a miracle he didn't die, much less that he wasn't paralyzed. He'd undergone surgery and had pins holding him together, but he was on both feet and healed.

And not shy about getting right back on his horse.

"Let's go."

Jack silently walked to Abacus, Broderick's well-mannered bay quarter horse. Clipping the leather lead line to the halter, he led Abacus to a crosstie.

With an anticipation he couldn't even begin to hide, Marshall slung the leather halter on his shoulder, moving toward the buckskin mustang. Flash's ears perked up, the dark brown of his mane contrasting with his cream-colored coat. Leading him out to the crossties behind Abacus, Marshall diligently brushed the horse down, losing himself in the routine of currycombing and hard brushing. Years and years of making horses his life afforded him the ability to quickly adapt to his injury.

Father and son moved in unison, saddling up in quiet synchronicity. As he tightened the girth, Flash let out a sigh, broad sides deflating, allowing Marshall to make a snug fit.

After sliding the bit into Flash's mouth, he took a deep breath. During his days on the rodeo circuit, the boys used to issue challenges to each other. One of them? Mounting into the saddle one-handed. He reached back to his younger years, knowing he could do it. Bracing his good hand on the saddle horse, he pulled himself up. Settling into the leather, he felt a helluva lot better.

Applying slight pressure to Flash's sides, he urged the horse forward to ride alongside Jack and Abacus. Golden rays of sunshine blanketed the snowy trail ahead of them.

Amid the sound of water lapping behind them and a stray call from a bird of prey, Marshall found conversation much easier. "Have you heard anything more from Shana on the investigation into finding Milla Jones?"

Jack adjusted the reins in his hand, guiding Abacus toward the tree line. "We're still in a holding pattern. She's hoping the DNA tests will reveal something useful."

"How's Jeannie doing with all of this?" Jeannie's youngest daughter—Alayna—had childhood memories come back of Jeannie's brother and sister and their possible involvement in a plot to harm the Steele family. It was difficult to know how much of the memory could be trusted since it had been repressed for so long, but it was unsettling regardless.

Marshall had known that blending longtime business rivals into one family would be challenging. But no one could have foreseen just how complicated it would become.

Although if Jack and Jeannie hadn't gotten married, would these secrets have stayed hidden? It was better knowing the truth.

Stillness found him. Steadied him. He'd needed this. All of this. Flash shook his mane. His horse also seemed to notice the way the sun set the icy water ablaze. Covered the snow in a golden glow.

Flash was a more even-paced horse than Marshall usually rode. The wind filtering through the expanse of land rustled leaves, bushes. Flash paid them no mind. No signs of spooking.

The creak of the saddle soothed his soul, giving him the bolstering he needed to say, "Dad, I've been keeping a secret from the family, and I think the time has come to let you all know."

His father shifted in the saddle, his eyes concerned. "This sounds serious. Whatever you need, I'm here for you."

"I know, and I haven't wanted to let you down."

Marshall forced his grip on the reins to loosen. "I'm a recovering alcoholic."

His father stayed quiet for a handful of heartbeats. "Thank you for telling me. What can I do to help?"

Marshall shook his head. "Just letting me get it off my chest means a lot to me. I've been dry for over four years, but I think the time has come to quit trying to fake people out with my bottles of nonalcoholic beers and tonic water."

"We're family, and I'm here for you whatever you need—Al Anon for family. You tell me."

Marshall swallowed hard, relief rolling the boulder off his shoulders. He hadn't even realized how heavily the secret had weighed on him until he was free of it.

Marshall lost himself in the movement of the ride, like a meditative rhythm.

"So, son, how're things with you and Tally?"

His father's intuitive question still caught Marshall off guard for moment. He sank deeper into the saddle, weighing his answer. "She's doing a great job getting the house ready for the fund-raiser."

"That's not what I mean—" his father shot him a sideways glance "—and I imagine you know it. I can't help but think she may have had something to do with what you've shared with me today."

"How did you guess?" Face growing taut, Marshall tightened his grip on the reins until the leather bit into his palm.

His father looked at him sidelong, the shade from his Stetson obscuring his eyes a bit. "It was impossible to miss the sparks flying off the two of you that day we were over decorating."

"She's a very special lady." And that was part of the problem. "I'm just not sure I can offer what she deserves."

"Why do you say that?"

"It's no secret I'm the loner in the family." His mount's ears perked up, rotating backward as if to eavesdrop.

"Just because you don't throw yourself into the thick of every gathering doesn't make you a loner. Your siblings have a way of taking over a room. You keep to the outskirts. No shame in that."

"That doesn't mean I'm right for Tally. She's so outgoing, far from being a loner like me."

"Not always. Your rodeo days included a full social circle."

Bad example. "Let's talk about something else."

Jack pushed Abacus into a working trot. Then to a rolling canter. They'd always had other ways of talking. Again, Flash's ears moved backward.

Marshall responded, squeezing his legs against Flash. His buckskin effortlessly transitioned to a smooth canter, and he found the mustang closing the distance on Abacus and his father.

Cool winter air and the rhythm of the ride opened him up. They reached the tree line and broke out into a walk.

Jack smiled, pivoting in the cognac-colored saddle to look at Marshall. He began to speak, sharing with Marshall a snippet of the past, a story he knew well. Once, the family went on a camping trip. Marshall, ever the curious adventurer, wandered off.

Jack continued, "It scared the hell out of me and your mother when we realized you weren't in your room. You were always so solitary. I wish I could say it was the first time we looked up and wondered where you were. Usually, you were in the old barn with the horse or just across the room with your nose in a book being so much quieter than the rest."

Marshall welcomed the distraction of his father's change of subject. "I played that up, you know. It gave me the chance to slip away."

"Do you remember where you were that day you wandered off in the snow?"

"I was building an ice fort. I must have been looking for a quiet space to read," he said with a smile. His parents and siblings had been making a gingerbread house. It had been chaos.

"You built it because Breanna asked you to. She wanted to have snowball fights where it wasn't boys against the girls, but where you were on her team."

"I'd forgotten that."

Jack reached down to give Abacus a pat on the neck. "You're a middle child in the way you keep to yourself and don't ask for what you need." Gathering the reins, he guided the bay quarter horse to the right. "For what my opinion's worth, I say if you want this woman, you should stop overthinking things and go for it. You're one helluva good man, and I would wager she sees that. Let her make her own decision. You're not responsible for the world."

Could it really be as simple as that? Was he over-thinking, as his father said? He wanted that to be true, to keep following the attraction and see where it led them.

And for that matter, he didn't need to make a decision until after the fund-raiser.

The prospect of being with Tally, guilt free, filled him with a thrill that rivaled anything he'd experienced, a new hope for the future with her. He ignored a niggling sense that Tally was hiding something. He was just overthinking things, like Jack said. Marshall was ready to embrace life and gear up for more from her.

Hell yes, he intended to fill their time together with romance—and desire.

Tally arranged and rearranged already perfectly spaced ornaments on the tree as if that could restore order to her life.

She needed to figure out a way to tell Marshall everything about her father. But with each passing day, it became tougher. Being with Marshall every morning and night had been a passionate fantasy come true.

From the speakers, the familiar notes of "Winter Wonderland" filled the air. Indeed. She felt those words. The sentiment. Her heart swelled in anxiety and ease all at once. This place—Marshall's home—was the stuff dreams were made of.

Looking around at the nativity scene, the twinkling lights on the tree, she almost felt at peace.

These were the holidays she dreamed of having. Wanted more than words. Her time here was about so much more than the job.

But before she could embrace even the thought of a future with Marshall, she would have to tell him everything.

Three successive rings disrupted her musing. Reaching into the pocket of her black skinny jeans, she retrieved her phone. Felicity's smiling face lit up the screen. Tally had taken the photo of Felicity when they'd gone for a short hike in the woods. The light filtering through the trees seemed to accent her friend's effortless, natural beauty.

With a smile on her face, Tally answered, "Hello, Felicity." She played with the ends of her hair, rubbing the strands between her fingers.

"Hi. I've missed our talks since little Stella Rae was moved out of the NICU."

"I've missed you, too. I'll be up there tomorrow if you're available to catch up."

"I would like that. I actually have a reason for calling. I wanted to share some information with you about a scholarship that came across my desk. Have you considered going back to school to become a social worker?"

Tally was honored that her friend would think of her, but had to say, "I don't think I could do your job."

"You're underestimating yourself. You're a natural in more ways than some people who've been on the job for years."

"I appreciate the vote of confidence. That means a lot to me."

"If you decide it's something you want to pursue, you know I'll help you however I can with a recommendation and finding the right college program for you."

She swallowed, envisioning her life as a social worker for a moment. What it would be like to intervene and give on that level? Tally felt her heart tighten. "Thank you. I'll give it some thought."

"I'm glad. No pressure, but the offer is genuine and real. Anyway—catch me up on your life."

"I've been meaning to ask you something. As I was leaving the hospital the other day, I could have sworn I saw you in the cafeteria eating with Conrad Steele."

A silence. Not a long one. But a noticeable one as Tally sank into the sofa, eyes trained on the fire in front of her.

"We ran into each other."

"Hmm, I'm finding maybe you're right about my instincts for counseling work, because I hear prevarication in your voice," she teased as she brought her knees to her chest, phone pressed to her ear.

"He's persistent," Felicity said tightly.

Tally wouldn't push Felicity before she was ready to share. Motion outside the window caught her attention—Marshall's vehicle coming up the drive. "I appreciate the call, and the information about the scholarship, thank you. Let's talk more tomorrow. I need to get back to work."

"Let's definitely do that. In person is always better." Felicity's voice echoed through the line. "Miss you. Can't wait to catch up more tomorrow."

"Me, too." Tally ended the phone call, eyes watching the window. To the dying light. To the whine of the SUV's engine as Marshall maneuvered to the garage and abruptly stopped short of it.

Flinging open the door, he sprinted out. Moving fast, a clear urgency in his steps because the SUV was still running. Concerned, she straightened, her attention homing in on him. Her eyes followed Marshall as he moved toward the older barn.

A glow lanced the darkening horizon. Not the haze of the sunset after all.

Flames shot from the older structure. The barn was on fire.

Ten

Marshall ran as fast as the snow would allow, his body acting on instinct. The old barn was on fire, and if it wasn't contained, the flames could spread to the main barn, where the animals were kept. He heard Tally shouting for him in the distance. He shot a quick look over his shoulder.

"Stay back," he barked.

Tally stood behind him, her open coat flapping in the evening wind. "I've called the fire department."

"Good," he said, his feet still on the move. He couldn't afford to wait around. "Get all the fire extinguishers from inside the house. I'll get the ones from the main barn."

He could also make a quick check on the animals

and ensure no sparks had found their way to the other structure. Hay ignited so damn fast.

But he couldn't mull over worst-case scenarios. He had too much to do. He raced into the main barn and gathered two fire extinguishers, relieved to see no signs of fire. The horses were restless, pawing at the ground, whinnying in distress. He hoped like hell none of them broke out of their stalls.

Plunging back into the snow, he clutched the fire extinguishers and raced toward the old barn. The original structure from back in his childhood.

The thought threatened to steal his focus.

He touched the door and found it cooler than he expected. A relief. Still, he needed to be careful of creating a back draft when he opened the barn door. Easing it open, staying well clear to the side, he assessed the interior. Sparks flew from the fuse box. Fire licked the ground around it, encroaching onto one of the old stalls.

The stall that had once held his childhood horse.

Marshall plunged inside, dropping one extinguisher and arming the other as he closed the distance. He foamed the flames, slowing the spread. The high ceilings kept the smoke at bay for now.

Just as the extinguisher spluttered on empty, the other was thrust into sight.

By Tally.

At some point, she'd joined him, staying silently back. Readying the next container. He took it gratefully from her hands and went to work on the remaining flames. With luck, he should be able to contain it until the fire department arrived and could soak it down to prevent a reignite.

As much as he wanted to tell Tally to leave, he knew she wouldn't. And he was grateful for her help.

Time felt distorted. As the fire continued to press onward, nothing made sense to him. He heard a siren sounding behind him, felt Tally's urgent hands pulling him back, but he didn't really understand that he needed to step back until one of the firefighters stood in front of him, shouting through his face mask to move away. His heart was beating wildly, and adrenaline coursed through every muscle in his body.

EMTs checked over both him and Tally, declaring them unharmed, attributing it to how quickly he'd subdued the flames and minimized the smoke. Marshall squeezed Tally's hand in comfort and quizzed the firefighters.

The general consensus was that the old fuse box had sparked with a surge, but an investigation would confirm that later.

Now, after the fire department had left, as Marshall checked on the horses in the main barn, everything he'd held at bay came flooding over him. He replayed the scene in his mind. The feeling of hopelessness as he watched the firefighters subdue the flames. Past and present collided in his mind. His mind still filled with images of the old barn on fire, a symbol of his childhood. His family. Going up in flames.

The gut punch of that chilled him still, reminding him what low reserves he had inside him for more loss.

The barn felt like a last sanctuary of the past. Of what life was like before. Before his mother and sister died. Before alcoholism took hold of him. Before the dark years. And now…his throat constricted. Air seemed impossible to swallow into his lungs.

Tally's light touch broke his thoughts. She wrapped him in a tight hug. "I'm so very sorry for what happened here."

The smell of smoke clung to her. Or maybe that was him.

For the first time he noticed the soot on his hands and jeans. "Insurance is there for a reason. It can be repaired."

But he knew it wouldn't look the same. Maybe the universe was pushing him to make those changes sooner rather than later.

"I'm sorry I didn't notice. I feel responsible for not catching it sooner. If you'd gotten home even a little later, this could have been very bad."

He swallowed, his eyes remaining unfocused. Looking at some invisible index of what was and all that was lost. "There's no way your eyes can be everywhere at once. I should have upgraded the barn sooner."

He'd been resistant to changing that place. And now it had cost him dearly. Even so, things could have been so much worse. At least no one had been hurt.

If Tally had gone down to the barn alone to battle the flames while he was gone… Even the unfinished thought made his gut clench. He should have had more farm staff on hand. This was his fault on so many levels.

Guilt stung hard and deep.

He wanted a drink.

At least there was no alcohol on the premises to tempt him in this weak moment. He would just climb into the shower and call this day over. In fact, showering and sleeping in the vacant bunkhouse was probably the wisest course of action. He could watch over the horses and ground himself again in the world where he felt most at home.

Tally rested a hand on his shoulder. "Are you okay?"

He flinched at her touch, his emotions so damn raw. "I'm fine. I'm relieved that you and the horses made it through unscathed."

"Because of you." Her voice was soft, the only other sound the snuffles of horses settling in for the night after the fright.

He wanted to take her, here and now. But after what she'd been through, his need felt selfish. Not to mention his control was shaky.

Marshall's heavy exhale ricocheted through his very core. The air tasted strange in his mouth. He needed to be useful. "Let me walk you back up to the house so you can get some rest."

"I don't want to rest. After the night we've had, my heart is in my throat. I want—I need—to be with you."

She stepped closer, sliding her arms around his

neck, leaning flush against him. There was no mistaking her intent and her certainty. His desire for her surged, riding the adrenaline still coursing through him.

With his reserves well below normal and needing to feel her vibrantly alive in his embrace, he couldn't find the will to tell her no.

Water from the bunkhouse shower rolled down Tally's body. Marshall stood against her, his cast in a plastic bag, his back taking the brunt of the spray. She could hardly believe all they'd been through together, working to keep the old barn safe until the fire department could arrive.

And they'd succeeded. Working side by side.

Adrenaline poured from her feet as surely as the water sluicing down and off her body. Cedar-planked walls of the bathroom created a warm, humid haven. Somehow, the scent of smoke and fire felt distant in this tiny room.

The immediate worries were past. Marshall had checked the animals over, and they appeared to be unharmed. But he'd put in a call to his farm veterinarian to look at them in the morning to make sure none had injured themselves in their stress. Thank goodness the integrity of the old structure had survived. It would require cleanup and repairs, but the barn was basically intact. It could have been so much worse.

She slid her arms around his waist, pressing her cheek to his chest, grateful he was unharmed. The stress in his tight muscles couldn't be ignored, and she couldn't blame him.

Her heart was still in her throat. She'd feared for his life as he'd worked to put the fire out. At least the animals had been secure in the main barn. Even after the fire department had arrived, they hadn't been able to stop Marshall from helping.

And for the first time, she wondered why he didn't have full-time ranch hands on staff. She'd noticed over her time working here that day workers came through to assist with feeding, riding and walking. Family assisted as well while he recovered. Still, the bunkhouse attached to the barn was empty even though he had the wealth to hire as much help as he chose.

This man was an island. And right now, she could see the weight of the world bearing down on his broad shoulders. And with everything that made him more honorable, she could only think of how that would make it all the more impossible for him to forgive her once he knew everything. The knife's edge of their time together coming to an end cut clean through her. Making her ache to take everything she could for as long as she could.

In a fluid motion, Marshall exited the shower, retrieving a massive fluffy white towel before slinging a second one around his waist. He wrapped her in the terry cloth, drawing her close to his chest. For a moment, they stayed locked together, still. Pressed against each other.

A deep breath filtered through her nose as her

skin touched his. Grabbing her hand, he led her toward the rustic four-poster bed made of sanded logs. He lowered her to the quilt before turning on the gas logs to further warm the main bedroom in the bunkhouse space.

The flames cast an amber glow over him, a reminder of the battle they'd waged together tonight. The earthy smell of the barn in keeping with the man she'd come to know so well over the past weeks. She'd learned every inch of him, but still reveled in exploring the hard planes of him. His body was the kind honed on the land and not in a gym.

She extended a hand to him. "Come join me."

"I intend to." He peeled the sleeve off his cast, then climbed onto the bed. The mattress gave with his weight as he settled beside her. He swept her wet hair away from her cheek. "Thank you again for your help earlier."

"I just followed your instructions."

His calm had been unbelievable. She'd been a bundle of nerves.

She still was.

Tally scooted closer and held him tight, her face buried in his neck. She inhaled the scent of soap lingering on his skin. He palmed her waist, his touch familiar now, but still so very stirring. His hand slid upward to cup the back of her head, and he eased away to skim his mouth over her jaw, up to her ears, then sealed his lips to hers.

The kiss exploded through her senses, unleashing all the tension inside her that had been building since she'd seen him walking toward the burning barn. He was alive, here in her arms, and she intended to celebrate in the most elemental way of all.

She lost herself in his kiss, the feel of his flesh against hers. She was so wrapped up in sensation, she barely registered him pressing her back into the pillows. His kisses trailed down to her collarbone, over her chest and lower, lower still, until… Her breath puffed free. He nudged her legs apart with his shoulders and gave her the most intimate of kisses.

He held her knees apart and nuzzled. Delicious sensation whispered through her. Her head pressed back into the pillow, and she gave herself over to him, a man she craved to know more about. He'd become all too important to her so quickly.

He stroked and tasted and guided her higher and higher, her breath carrying husky moans of encouragement. His calloused hands held her thighs, and she reveled in the raspy texture of him.

Her release crashed over her again, and again, tension from the evening rippling away on each pleasurable spasm.

Then he inched up her body, rolling her to her side until they faced each other. His cast arm rested over her waist. His eyes glowed in the night.

He reached for his jeans on the floor and pulled his wallet from the back pocket. He withdrew a condom, and she was grateful to him for remembering to take care. He sheathed himself, then eased her leg up over his hip, pressing inside her.

Instinct and sensation took over as she welcomed

him into her body. She met him thrust for thrust. Nerve endings tingled to life, simmering and singing through her.

Their hips rolled against each other, his injured arm a sturdy weight against her waist, needing this, needing *him* after the night they'd been through.

He breathed against her ear. "I can't wait to get this cast off and make love to you unfettered."

"I have no complaints." She kissed droplets of water from his chest.

"And I intend to keep it that way," he murmured against her ear.

He angled his mouth over hers, their lovemaking intensifying, every time better than the last as they learned more about bringing each other to the edge of bliss and back again. The heat and glide of his body against hers stirred the tension in her higher again, bringing her close to completion a second time. Sweat slicked their bodies as they moved against each other. The musky scent of him and their passion made for a heady perfume, and she couldn't get enough.

His head dipped to nuzzle her neck, her collarbone, her breasts. Her hands roved over him, stroking the hard planes of his honed body. Her head fell to rest on his shoulder, her teeth sinking in lightly. His husky growl of approval rumbled against her. Her emotions were so raw and elemental tonight, and their coming together mirrored that.

Each rock of their hips against each other stoked bliss richer and fuller through her. Her eyes squeezed closed as she held tight to him, to the sensation coursing through her, building until…sparks shimmered behind her eyelids. Her back arched into her completion, her fingers sinking into his shoulders.

She felt his orgasm power through him, and she reveled in knowing she gave him the same pleasure he brought her. As the aftermath simmered through her, he gathered her against his chest, his hands gentle along her hypersensitive skin.

Her forehead pressed to his neck, she couldn't hide from the fear any longer. Having something happen to Marshall tonight would have rattled her world, too much. She couldn't pretend this was casual, not any longer.

Her time to hold back the past from him had come to an end.

The next morning, Marshall buried himself in routine after the vet left, so much to be done in the aftermath of the fire. He and Tally had slept in the bunkhouse through the night, waking with just enough time to throw on fresh clothes before his siblings and the veterinarian arrived.

After he let his family know about the fire, Jack and Jeannie had sent along a message that they had a meeting to attend but would be by as soon as they finished.

With thoroughness characteristic of his family's love of their animals, Marshall was determined to examine each horse personally. His veterinarian, Dr. Cibou, had issued clean bills of health. Still,

Marshall needed to see with his own eyes. His older brother, Broderick, assisted, bringing each horse to Marshall, holding the still-flighty horses steady as Marshall checked.

He'd left his other siblings scattered throughout the damaged structure and back at the house. Tally gave him a curt nod, busying herself in the kitchen, making enough food to feed his large family. Light snowfall dimmed the scorches on the barn, but the area still smelled of smoke.

Broderick clasped a lead line with ease, stroking underneath the mane of a sorrel horse. "Are you sure you don't need to go to the doctor?"

Marshall skimmed his hand on the sorrel's hind-quarters, down to the fetlock. The sorrel lifted his foot in response. Marshall wanted to be sure no glass or debris had been picked up and become lodged in the horse's hooves.

"I was checked out by the paramedics last night." Marshall pressed around, checking for sensitivity. Nothing. Another sigh of slight, bittersweet relief.

"Just be careful. You're not immortal."

"Don't I know it." He held up his cast arm. "I'm about ready to saw this cast off like I did when I was a kid."

"Mom was so mad at you." Broderick led the sorrel away, turning him out into the pasture. The horse trotted out to the small herd of animals that had already been screened.

"I had to read Aiden an extra bedtime story every night that summer. The brat chose the longest books he could find. I thought it was by accident until I caught him comparing the length. Although I didn't really mind because I love books, which Mom knew all along."

Broderick laughed softly. "She was wise that way." He clapped his brother on the shoulder. "It'll all work out. The insurance will cover the rebuild. But it's going to be chaos. We'll house some of the livestock at Dad's place until things settle down."

Broderick brought a palomino forward. The golden coat shimmered in the sun. Little snowflakes clung to the horse. The mare looked enchanted. Calmest one yet. Marshall began his exam again. Muscle memory guiding him, keeping exhaustion at bay.

"I blame myself for this whole mess. If I hadn't been so damn stubborn about not having a hand living in the bunkhouse, there would have been someone there." He scratched the horse behind the ear. The mare's long neck stretched, leaning into the affection.

"Accidents happen. There are plenty of ranches that don't have round-the-clock staff. That said, you don't have to run the place on your own."

He nodded tightly.

A car engine's purr echoed in the barn. The engine cut off, replaced by quick footfalls on gravel and snow. Their father, Jack, rounded the corner into the barn. His hands in thick gloves, he wiped his snow-flecked hair. "Can you boys come inside? We have something we need to tell the family."

Their father sounded serious, but before Marshall could question him, Jack had already left.

Broderick and Marshall finished examining the palomino mare quickly and silently. His father was not one for dramatic scenes.

Marshall made his way with his older brother to the house, falling a few steps behind his kid brother, Aiden. His youngest brother glanced over his shoulder, deep lines of worry on his teenage face.

The short trek from the barn gave Marshall space to breathe for a moment. The snowfall became a mess of footsteps. Hunting had never been his strongest skill, but he did note the chaos of the imprints in the snow. People moved with speed into the house. Aiden held the door for his brothers, and they hurried into the dining room.

Tally's red hair, drawn back into a ponytail, bobbed as she finished setting down a platter of sandwiches beside a chafing dish full of stew. She smoothed her emerald green long-sleeve shirt, catching Marshall's eye. Felt the warmth radiate from her gaze. "I'll be in the kitchen if anyone needs anything."

Marshall held out an arm for her. "Stay. Join us."

Jack and Jeannie exchanged pointed looks before Jack nodded. "Yes, Tally. If Marshall wants you to stay, then please do. This won't be a secret for long, anyway."

With a small nod, she closed the distance between them, moving to his side. He half expected her now-familiar light touch to his arm. But her hands remained in front of her.

For a moment, this scene felt familiar. Memories of family meetings in this room danced before his eyes. This is where he'd found out he'd be an older brother.

The gathering today had a similar feel, except there were stepchildren and spouses here as well now. And there'd been a time long ago when he had gathered the family in this very spot. He'd sat in Tally's seat, a notebook filled with plans. At ten years old, he had tried to convince his father to let him run the barrels at the largest rodeo in the area. Marshall had presented his plan with a cool efficiency. A lighthearted meeting in retrospect, but the presentation had seemed life-or-death back then.

The expression on Jack's face was far from lighthearted.

Marshall frowned. "What's wrong?"

Jack dropped into the chair; his broad shoulders, normally so square and strong, seemed deflated. He rested his hands on his knees. "I know this is a bad time with what happened last night in the barn, but this can't wait." He drew in a ragged breath, his face haggard. "Shana had a development in the investigation into Milla Jones's disappearance."

Marshall was stunned silent. The statement sounded like a foreign language he could not quite grasp, his ears ringing while his siblings blurted questions in rapid-fire succession.

"Have you found her?" Broderick demanded, hand fiddling with the plate before him.

Naomi's face turned grave, rage filling her eyes. "Where is she?"

"Why did she run?" Aiden demanded, leaning forward in his seat.

Jack held up a hand to silence them before continuing. "She hasn't been found. But the DNA results from the brush she left revealed some…shocking results."

Marshall found his voice again. "What do you mean?"

"She isn't who she claimed to be."

Naomi's lip curled. "That's no surprise. She was deceitful from the start."

Jack leveled a somber gaze at his children that started a roar of premonition in Marshall's head. "You need to prepare yourself." He paused, his shoulders bracing, his haggard face pulling tighter. "Her DNA is a match to…Breanna's."

Gasps filled the room. Broderick's legs went out from under him and he sank into a chair, his wife's arm going around him. The roaring in Marshall's brain intensified. Joy and denial mixing in a wash of confusion and betrayal. In a dim corner of his consciousness he realized Tally had slid her hand into his and was holding on tightly.

His jaw tense, Jack rubbed a hand behind his neck. "It appears this 'Milla' was telling the truth about Breanna being alive after all, because *she* is our Brea."

Eleven

Tally wanted to comfort Marshall, but even an hour after his family had cleared out, she didn't know how to reach through the wall around him. He was going through the motions of finishing up with the horses, putting them back into the main barn.

So much had happened in such a short time, her world felt off-kilter. She'd couldn't imagine how he must feel.

After cleaning away the last of the untouched food—no one had felt much like eating after the announcement about Brea—Tally closed the refrigerator and sagged back to rest against the stainless steel.

Why would Breanna pretend to be someone else and keep her identity from the family? It didn't make sense. They'd loved her. She'd loved them. Where had she been all these years?

So many torturous questions and too few answers.

And in the middle of it all, Tally had a dilemma of her own. Her father had been a part of whatever happened all those years ago with the plane crash. Even if his part had been unintentional, the crash had happened—and not in the way people believed. If knowing about her father's role that day could somehow shed even a hint of light on what happened, Tally couldn't hold it back from the family anymore.

As much as she ached to give Marshall space to come to grips with what he'd learned, what if delaying further gave Milla/Brea more time to fade away? Whatever her reason for doing so?

Guilt knotted Tally's gut over not having come clean sooner. She'd been selfish, thinking only of holding on to Marshall and what they shared for as long as possible.

She was falling for him. Hard. And even if she hadn't, she owed him the truth. All of it.

Her insides quivering with nerves and yes, fear, she sat at the table and waited for him to return. Eyes glued on the front door, she popped a pen cap on and off. Set the pen down on the table. Picked it up again as if routine and ritual alone would make her conversation easier. Manageable.

Wind bellowed, whipping through the house as Marshall finally crossed the threshold. Snow clung to his wispy dark hair and clothes. Wordlessly, he peeled off his coat and boots. The air still retained a biting cold. A cold that nipped at the pit of Tally's stomach.

He made his way into the kitchen, socks muffling his footfalls. He barely glanced at the kitchen island. Went straight to the stainless steel refrigerator. With the weight of the world in his eyes, he pulled out a water bottle. "What a long damn day."

It wasn't that long ago that he'd been there for her—supporting her wordlessly after she'd had a hellish day. She wished she could return that favor now, and hated that she was about to complicate matters more.

The pen cap wore a groove in her thumb as she continued to push the cap on and off. Deciding to tell him didn't make it any easier. "Um, yes, it has been. Did you get the horses all secure for the night?"

"They're all bedded down." To Tally's eye, Marshall seemed to be searching. Trying to locate something in his kitchen that kept eluding him. He touched the stones on the island for a moment, walked across the room to open a cabinet. Tally's throat felt bone-dry. "I should probably call it a day, too. Are you coming up?"

She clutched the edges of the table. "I need to tell you something."

"That sounds ominous. I'm not sure I have it in me for more shocks today," he said with a half smile.

She wanted to wait, to steal one more night with him, but that wouldn't be fair to anyone. "It's…

difficult. And I should have told you sooner. Could you please sit down?"

Frowning, he sank into a chair beside her, his water bottle in one hand. "I'm listening."

"It's about what happened to your mother and your sister."

He sat up straighter, setting the bottle aside. "What do you mean?"

"My father was an airplane mechanic. His drinking got worse because he felt responsible for a fatal crash." She swallowed hard. "He was the mechanic responsible for the aircraft that went down with your mother and sister on board."

The truth hurt her as she spoke it. She couldn't begin to imagine the pain it caused him.

He studied her through narrowed eyes. "You've known this since you came to work here?"

His words came out slowly, carefully.

She nodded. "I was hoping to find some kind of closure to what caused my father to take his life. I came here with the intent to tell you, when the time was right. And I've finally realized there could never be a perfect time to share this."

Shock in his eyes, he stared at her, his body still. "And even when I told you there was some kind of question about whether or not my sister survived, you didn't think it might be worth mentioning?"

"I didn't want to cause you further stress, which I know sounds like a cop-out now," she rushed to add, "but it made sense at the time."

She could see him closing down, shutting her

out. The spark that used to be visible in his eyes when he looked at her was gone. It was too much for him—the barn, his sister. He should be celebrating that she might be alive, and instead Tally was heaping this on him.

She'd let him down by not telling him sooner. And they were both paying the price in her timing now.

He eased back in his chair. "I want to believe you. But there's also a part of me that's wondering if you're telling me now because you think since my sister is alive it doesn't matter."

"That's not it at all." She reached out to touch his wrist, wishing she could reclaim this pain between them. Lessen it, at least. He flinched, but didn't pull away. "The time was never…"

She searched for the right words and realized there were none. She had no justification. "Fine. You're right. I have no excuse. I came here for the job, hoping to get ahead while making peace with my past."

She'd been selfish, wrong.

And she saw the betrayal burning in his eyes.

Tally eased her hand away from him. "I'll pack my things and leave."

"No," he said tightly, standing. "You were hired to do a job. I'm not going to penalize my family for our mistakes. See the fund-raiser event through, and then you can consider your employment complete."

She couldn't stop herself from making a last-ditch effort. "Can we talk about this?"

"There's nothing more to say." He picked up his coat. "I'm going to sleep in the bunkhouse to watch over the horses."

Turning on his heel, she saw his guard go all the way up as his muscled back tensed. He moved toward the door, deadly silent. Tally watched him sling on his coat and boots.

A low whistle called Nugget from slumber. The little dog kept close to his human, though the pup gave a backward glance before the door shut. Marshall left her alone.

Just like that.

A world, a future, everything gone.

He shut her out, becoming as impossibly distant as an island far away from shore. She had no boat, no oar, nothing to reach him with.

She felt the gulf between them, felt alone in the world again, too. Quicker than the fire that claimed his old barn, she'd torched any tender feelings between them forever. Tally set the pen down atop her to-do list.

Neatly. Precisely. She adjusted the angle. Her world was spinning out of control. And all she could do to hold on was her job, prepare for the fund-raiser, then pack her few things.

Salty tears brimmed in her eyes, threatening to release a deluge of hurricane proportions. Throat bobbing, she put a hand to her forehead, hoping to stay the tears.

She had no more words. Nothing she could say

could intervene now. Peace was nowhere to be found.

This fairy tale had come to an abrupt end. The bond—that connection—was snipped forever.

Lingering scents of fire and ash still permeated the bunk room. Or perhaps they still clung to his jacket. Destruction all around him in little and profound ways.

Nugget ran around the bunk room, tail wagging. A sad smile pulled his cheek muscles upward. He wished for the dog's unbridled ease.

Stripping down to a white T-shirt and boxers, Marshall crawled into bed. Nugget jumped on the mattress after him, circling three times before settling against Marshall's left side.

Absently, his eyes flitted around the bunk room, catching on the sturdy exposed wood. With a deep inhale, his nostrils were filled with memories. Scents of Tally permeated the sheets.

His hold on sobriety was teetering on the edge. He was one breath away from four years down the tubes. He'd thought he could tackle giving a future with Tally a try, but he'd been wrong on so many levels. His feelings for her overwhelmed him, as if he'd become addicted.

The chilly air rasped in his throat. Burned his lungs. His head throbbed as if he suffered from a hangover after hitting rock bottom. He felt the pit of his addiction roil beneath the surface.

Weeks ago, he'd been fine on his own. Managed

this whole place alone. Kept the world at bay. Then Tally came into his life with a literal splash.

Moving through the days with her had been so damn easy, like they'd known each other for far longer. His fingers ached for the now-familiar feeling of her soft skin.

Only, everything they'd shared together had been based on a lie.

Hell yes, he was raw from knowing she'd lied to him from the start of working here, but there was more to it than that. He hadn't seen it. He'd been 100 percent blind when it came to her. Now? How could he possibly trust himself or his judgment? Sure, he'd been a man battling addiction when Tally had shown up. But at least he'd been keeping his head above water, dealing with it.

The punch to his gut that she'd delivered threatened to pull him under for good. And he could not let it, no matter how much losing her was going to hurt. He needed to be stronger than that now. He needed to draw in tight and hold on to his self control. He owed it to his family, to his mother's memory and to his sister. Whatever had driven Brea away, she would need her family stronger than ever when they found her. He couldn't afford a lapse now.

His whole family would need to be stronger than ever for whatever they would find.

And even as he reasoned through everything that had crashed in on his life in a short twenty-four hours, he couldn't avoid the deep-seated truth. No matter how much Tally had come to mean to him, someone like him, fighting such dark demons on a daily basis, couldn't be the right man to bring the light into her world that she deserved.

Tally found the Christmas spirit tough to salvage, going through the motions.

Even when things with her father were at their worst, Christmas week held the potential for magic. The dark years after his suicide were lonely, sure, but she had always managed to find some small cheer in service to others.

Touching her sterling silver necklace, she attempted a smile, some pretense of enjoying herself for the benefit of the fund-raiser. The event was in full swing. The main house was being used for food and socializing. Later, everyone would ride in horse-drawn sleighs to the barn for the bachelor auction. It had been a crunch getting the old barn repaired in time to house the horses so the main barn could be used for the event, but they'd pulled it off. Marshall and his family had worked tirelessly.

Everything was dazzling. And her heart was in tatters.

She didn't know how she'd made it through the past three weeks getting ready for the fund-raiser, a cold silence between her and Marshall. He'd moved into the bunkhouse, which felt so surreal. She was the hired help living in his mansion and he'd retreated to the barn.

He'd also hired more help during the day, which had put a buffer between them as they'd each gone about their jobs. And now, even their stilted time together was coming to an end. There would be no happy ending for them.

Lump still in her throat, Tally did her best to present a professional face. She wore a smile as another accessory, a complement to the simple black dress.

Across the room, the Mikkelson and Steele clans mingled, giving all appearances of a blended, tight family for the benefit of the business. Snippets of conversation punctuated the room. The gathering was modest in size, but not in terms of the guest list. Key figures from Alaska and the Pacific Northwest chatted with the Alaska Oil Barons. This event attracted old, big money to commemorate the newly formed Steele/Mikkelson Charity Foundation.

Felicity squeezed her hand, her glimmering eyes reflecting the twinkling white lights. "You've done an amazing job pulling this off. If you decide not to be a social worker, you could definitely be one helluva party planner."

"I'm just focused on the present for now."

Tally shivered, her dress rippling against her skin. She smoothed the front of her floor-length black gown to be the picture of elegance and class, to give this final gift to Marshall in making the party a success. If she could appear the part of a cool, collected hostess, maybe he wouldn't notice the way sadness settled in her soul.

Felicity shot her a sidelong glance, those knowing brows arching. She crossed her arms over her chest, drawing tight the shimmery emerald fabric of her gown. "Are you okay?"

No. The opposite of okay. Not that Tally would admit as much. Even talking about it could well make her fall to pieces. "I'm fine. I'm finishing my job here, then I'll be moving on to the next."

"And you and Marshall?"

The question hurt so much more than it should have. "There is no me and Marshall."

"But there was," Felicity prodded gently.

"Not anymore." If Tally had been honest with him from the start, maybe. But there was no going back. She wanted peace and went about it in all the wrong ways.

Felicity hooked an arm through hers and squeezed. "Ah, hon, I'm so sorry."

"Me, too. I have no one to blame but myself."

Tally's eyes followed Marshall as he stood with his family. The Steeles and Mikkelsons had on their best social faces, but she could see the strain in their expressions. No further news had come through about his missing sister, and she couldn't imagine the torture they were enduring.

She hated that she'd brought any more pain to them. What had she been thinking coming here in the first place, intruding on their grief? The guilt was crushing, so much so she had an inkling of what her father must have felt.

Ever the compassionate soul, Felicity's voice lowered. She fixed her eyes softly on Tally. "Do you want to talk about it?"

"Not really. Just enjoy the party."

A symphony of laughter erupted from across the room. An Alaskan senator wiped tears of laughter from his eyes, clutching his glass of champagne. Tally just wanted to lose herself in work, finish this evening, then curl up in her room and unleash the flood of tears.

"For what my opinion's worth, that man is crazy about you. I'm not a success story by a long shot— my marriage was a disaster." Pain pinched at Felicity's face for a moment before she continued, "But from where I'm standing, Marshall hasn't taken his eyes off you all evening. Someone who works that hard to stay away usually does so because of strong feelings."

Could he really still care for Tally? Or was that just wishful thinking? Felicity was a professional at reading people, the skill integral to her job. Tally wanted to trust her.

If only she knew how to bridge the gap. She'd been on her own for so long, and she'd risked her heart on Marshall. Before she'd even known what was happening, she'd fallen for him hard, and now she was so empty inside she echoed.

Was there something she was missing? A tactic she hadn't tried to heal the rift between them? Even if it meant losing him forever as her lover, she'd trade anything to at least part as...*friends* seemed too tame a word.

But she couldn't bear to think of Marshall Steele as her enemy, either. She needed help. Because she still needed peace and couldn't leave until she found it somehow.

A Christmas sign would be more than welcome, even if she'd given up hope in miracles.

Twelve

Felicity had never imagined she would be attending a bachelor auction.

But since the new charity foundation had listed child services as one of its causes, she needed to make an appearance. And truth be told, she found the notion of Conrad on the catwalk to be something she didn't want to miss.

The dinner portion of the Mikkelson-Steele charity fund-raiser had concluded. The partiers had relocated to the barn for the bachelor auction.

Tally stood next to her, red hair falling in loose, romantic curls. If she didn't know her friend better, she would have assumed Tally was happy. She certainly kept a ready smile in place.

Years of training told Felicity otherwise. Her

friend's relentlessly straight shoulders spoke volumes about the tension she was feeling. Pain radiated from her.

Risk and trust were close cousins. They accompanied each other. Sometimes they did damage together. A fact she knew all too well.

And a fact that caused Felicity unease of her own. She watched Conrad button his tuxedo jacket. He caught her eye, gave her a wink.

Conrad moved quickly with determination and charm. His romance game unsettled her, scared her. The wounds of her failed marriage still stung. For all her skill with communication and people, she couldn't seem to find the words to tell her appealing suitor that things needed to move slower. Why couldn't he understand given his own relationship failures?

The auctioneer for the event cleared his throat, effectively extinguishing the conversation in the room. Felicity looked at the runway. Tally had a hand in helping the event come together. Her friend had hung heart-shaped snowflake formations from the barn's rafters. Faux snow blanketed the runway. Tall, skinny pine trees decorated the back of the stage. A mini winter wonderland.

Conrad walked down the runway. Slow, determined strides. Women in the audience murmured about his sexy, tight-lipped half smile. A bidding war began between a bleached-blonde woman in a gown of sapphire and a brunette in a deep burgundy. Cheering erupted as the women drove Conrad's price higher and higher.

Deep in Felicity's stomach, a pang of jealousy bubbled. She had no claim, no right to the emotion and no room in her life for romance. She didn't have the emotional reserves to risk another heartbreak.

With a deep breath, she did her best to not be distracted by how downright handsome Conrad looked in his custom-fitted tuxedo. The blonde raised her paddle, and the woman in red tapped out. The auctioneer almost called it until Naomi Steele, one of Conrad's nieces, shot her paddle into the air, upping the bid substantially. The blonde shook her head.

The auctioneer nodded, attributing the bet to...

"Felicity Hunt."

Felicity stifled a gasp through sheer willpower. All eyes turned to her. Anger iced her. She knew a setup when she saw it. And Conrad had very clearly maneuvered this to push forward his agenda.

Conrad descended from the runway, heading toward where she and Tally were seated at the back of the rows of chairs. For a brief moment, Felicity felt like a hypocrite, turning away, needing to put space between herself and the admittedly sexy man. It didn't matter that she'd just spouted romantic encouragement to her friend Tally. Felicity wasn't in the market for following her own advice, for being open to deeper feelings.

The truth was, as much as she'd hoped she could indulge in a light relationship with this man, she just wasn't ready. Her divorce had left her too raw.

Practically out the door, or at least around the corner, Felicity searched for her coat-check ticket so she could leave. She needed to get out of this barn with all its confusing tensions. Conrad closed the distance between them, cornering her just outside the tack room, out of sight from the rest of the crowd.

"Is everything okay?"

Felicity wanted to say yes and just walk away, but she'd never been any good at lying. "You orchestrated that winning bid."

"I thought you would find the gesture romantic."

And perhaps it was. But she couldn't allow this flirtation to continue. "It doesn't matter now. What's done is done. Might as well make the best of it."

"Other men might be insulted by the horror in your voice," he said dryly.

"I'm more frustrated with myself. I think I've given you the wrong impression with our lunches." Felicity searched for the right words to put an end to this in a diplomatic way, but above all to be upfront and honest. "I just want to make sure you understand. I've already suffered through a divorce. It was a hell I'm not interested in repeating."

"As I've said before, we're not talking about getting married. We were discussing a date." He arched a brow.

She was starting to feel foolish. Had she read too much into his attention? "I'll honor the bid, but to be fair, I'm not at a place where I'm ready to let someone into my life."

"You don't plan to date? Or remarry? You're planning to live a nun's life, taking care of orphans?"

She didn't like his tone of voice one bit. "And if that's my plan, what's so wrong with it?"

"I could swear I saw interest in your eyes." He clasped her shoulders, drawing her near.

"That's why I'm not officially a nun." She tipped her face defiantly, wanting to kiss him, to lose herself in his embrace. But just as she couldn't lie to him, she also couldn't lie to herself.

There could never be anything simple between them. The draw was too potent. Too powerful.

"And you're not interested in taking a risk?"

"No, I'm not." She infused her voice with resolution, because if she weakened at all and he noticed... She wasn't sure how long she could hold out.

Sighing, he stepped back, the air crackling between them with desire and regret. "Damn shame. We could have had something special." Conrad straightened his tie. "No worries about going on the date. I'll use the purchased time to volunteer somewhere like the hospital. Just say where your office needs the help most."

She watched him disappear into the crowd, and even knowing she'd made the right decision, she wondered what might have happened if she'd met him a decade earlier.

Marshall thrust his hand through his hair, the bow tie damn near choking him.

Still, his least favorite part of the fund-raiser was

complete—the bachelor bid. It had been difficult for him to parade around on the best days. It had been far harder knowing Tally was in the audience, watching. The winning bid had been a grand dame whose family were major sponsors of bringing rodeos to town. She'd bought his promotional presence.

At least he didn't have to navigate the waters of an awkward date. His eyes were drawn to Tally, her elegance and poise.

Live music hung in the air, a song about love at Christmastime. His jaw taut, he did his best to stay anchored. Marshall had gone to an AA meeting and spent an extra hour with his sponsor prior to tonight, shoring himself up on so many levels.

Naomi's husband, Royce, made his way to Marshall. The Alaska Oil Barons, Inc.'s environmental scientist looked at the cluster of people and did his best to walk by without being bogged down in idle conversation. Marshall assumed that as a reclusive, introverted and brilliant scientist, Royce was probably as eager to finish up this party as he was.

Naomi's husband leaned against a barn beam. "You've been hugging the wall mighty hard tonight."

Marshall sipped his sparkling water and looked out on the crowd, where the waitstaff seamlessly weaved through the long gowns and winter floral arrangements, filling drinks for the guests engaged in deep conversation. He flickered his eyes to Royce. "I'm here. I've fulfilled the family's wishes. It's no secret the news about Breanna has rocked us all."

He hadn't been able to get his feet back under him since that day. He'd carried on, of course, getting ready for this event. And the charity fund-raiser had clearly succeeded. The bachelor auction brought in a good deal of money, and other donations were already being made by impressed and intrigued guests. Judging by the sounds of the conversation, the party would continue for a time.

"How are you coping?" Royce tapped Marshall's glass and pinned him with a look.

No need to hide the truth any longer. "Did Dad tell you?"

Marshall had been meaning to get the word out, but with everything that had happened with Brea, and then Tally, he hadn't gotten around to it.

A waiter came by with a plate of appetizers— smoked salmon, avocado and cucumber. Tally had done a good job finding foods that appealed to everyone tonight. Both Royce and Marshall snagged some of the food.

Marshall popped the treat in his mouth, bracing himself for discussion about his alcoholism.

"No," Royce said. "I only had a suspicion. You just confirmed it. Jack knows?"

Marshall swirled his glass in time to "O Holy Night." Shaking his head, a ragged sigh escaped his lips. Every new person to know simultaneously alleviated the burden and highlighted his struggle. "I told him a few weeks ago. I planned to tell the rest of the family, but with the news about Breanna, I haven't gotten around to it. Who else suspects?"

"No one's heard it from me. So I'll ask again, how are you handling the news?"

Not well, afraid as hell to hope his sister could really be alive. Finding it tough to look into the future. "You said it yourself—I'm hugging the wall."

"Reaching out might be more beneficial."

Marshall snorted on a laugh. "You're one to talk."

"Exactly," Royce said, going silent for a moment. Marshall could see his brother-in-law process his thoughts. "I've existed on the outskirts of people's lives for a very long time. It can be a lonely place even in a crowd."

The words cut through him. Forever grateful for AA, Marshall knew what looking for support meant. What it was like to find someone reliable. As he chewed on Royce's words, his eyes instinctively drifted toward where Tally stood, chatting in a small circle of people.

Royce clapped him on the shoulder. "I'm lucky I found Naomi. Because sometimes support isn't about having twenty people to talk to. It's about having one right person who really gets you."

The scientist strode off, melting into the crowd, making Marshall wonder for a moment if the guy had intended to give him romantic advice, or if his timing had been a matter of luck. A little bit of Christmas cheer where he'd least expected it.

Because his brother-in-law had a point.

A knowing rose in his chest as he gazed at Tally. She had been there for him, since that first day she'd jumped in his pool to rescue his dog. She'd supported him and really listened to him. Yet he'd turned her away. Sure, he wished she'd told him everything sooner, but no one was perfect. Damn ironic that he, of all people, would forget that for a single minute.

He needed to show her how important she was to him. Hell, how much he loved her.

He just hoped he wasn't too late.

Sixteen hours ago, Tally had moved through the Steele-Mikkelson charity event in a daze. Even now, she remembered the night in flashes of dreamlike images and feelings. Marshall's face, his distance, her regret.

Her own regret over not having found a way to be honest with him sooner.

This morning, she found solace in the routine of the hospital. Tomorrow was Christmas Eve, and her contract working for the Steeles would come to a close. She still needed to make one more trip back to Marshall's house to pack and clear out before the family's holiday, and she dreaded that with a deep, slicing grief.

For now, she would remain here in the moment. Present. Focused on baby Erica in her arms. Gently rocking the sweet girl back and forth as hospital staff milled about checking charts. One of her favorite nurses waved at Tally, green eyes bright in spite of having to work over the holidays, in spite of the critically ill children all around. The nurse wore scrubs patterned with tiny wreaths. A silver tinsel tree was parked in a corner. Little touches to make the next few days more bearable for the families.

The infant in her arms neared sleep. Her eyes fluttered shut. Tally smiled down at her charge, blinking back tears for fear the relatives might see them.

From the corner of her eye, a movement caught her attention. Not the normal traffic of nurses and doctors. Something else. Through the large window, she saw familiar broad shoulders approaching the nurses' station.

Marshall.

What was he doing here? No matter, he stole her breath in his simple red plaid shirt and jeans, wide belt buckle gleaming. Then she noticed he carried a large box filled with ornately wrapped gifts.

The staff clustered around him, their tired expressions replaced with smiles as he pulled out presents for staff, parents and children. Did she dare hope he'd done this for her? And even if he hadn't, the kind of man who would make this thoughtful gesture was a person of honor, integrity. A man worth fighting for. Her eyes filled with tears.

Rising from the rocker, Tally lowered the sleeping infant into the bassinet. Touching the infant's little hand, her heart swelled. She thought of her own child preparing for Christmas, a life she honored by being here even knowing she would carry the ache of loss forever. Marshall carried burdens of his own, and rather than letting them break him, he tackled them head-on every day. She admired him for that.

She turned back to the window. Pace and pulse quickening as her eyes fell on Marshall. He stood, waiting. Their eyes met. Connected.

Hope churning inside her, she passed through the door.

"Hello, Tally, care to take a walk?" He extended an arm.

She noticed his cast was gone. She took his arm and walked beside him, the warmth of him familiar and welcome after their estrangement. She'd missed him, so very much.

Words failed her as they meandered, winding their way through the hospital until they came upon a small meditation garden. The enclosed structure allowed sunlight to stream through, lighting the rock path winding through flowering plants. Sprawling greenery filled the space with summer in winter, a fountain spewing in the center with a soothing *shoosh* of water. And as luck would have it, the space was empty, giving them privacy to talk.

He guided her to a bench and sat beside her. "I appreciate your talking to me."

"I appreciate what you did for the children—for the families and staff, too." The image of him passing out gifts still filled her mind and heart. "That was so thoughtful of you."

Writing a check was easy. Showing up was harder.

He took her hand in his, his thumb stroking along the inside of her wrist. "It's my Christmas gift to you—along with my apology."

That he'd chosen something he knew would make her happy touched her all the more.

She flipped her hand in his, linking their fingers, taking hope from the warmth in his eyes. "If anyone should apologize, it's me."

"Thank you, but no." He pressed a finger to her lips. "I should have never let things go this long without talking to you. I shut you out, and that was wrong."

"I shouldn't have lied to you," she insisted.

"And I shouldn't have lost my temper."

It was about more than that, and she couldn't shy away from it. "I should have told you about my father. You had every right to be upset."

"What happened with your father was an accident," he said with unmistakable certainty, his gaze steady and strong. "He paid a high price for his feelings of guilt... So did you."

"Your family paid a much higher price."

His hold tightened on hers. "Life isn't easy. Having you in my life has taught me I can't isolate myself. That's no way to honor my mother's memory. And it certainly hasn't taken away the pain of losing them. Having you here made me realize I should be opening my life, not closing it off."

His words touched her with hope, for him as much as for her. She liked the idea of this amazing man rejoining the world with all he had to offer.

She slid her hands to cup his face. "You credit me with too much."

"You don't credit yourself with enough." He covered her hands with his. "But I want to be around, in your life, to tell you every day just how damn special you are."

Her heartbeat skittered faster, her breath catching with surprise and more of that heady sensation of hope.

"That easily, you forgive me?"

He rested his forehead against hers. "Yes, and I hope you'll forgive me."

His scent, his nearness, soothed an ache in her that went far beyond the past few unhappy weeks. He eased her soul in a deeper way than that, filling her with a sense of rightness.

"Of course I do."

His eyes filled with something that looked remarkably like love. "And what if I said I want us to continue seeing each other? Because the thought of letting you go is driving me insane." He clasped her shoulders, his touch stirring her the way it always had, and more. "Tally, I'm falling head over heels in love with you."

Joy filled her to overflowing, just like that garden fountain. It seemed to spill right out of her along with a few happy tears.

"I'm so very glad to hear that, because I'm right there with you." Happiness curled deep inside her, like it was ready to stay for a long, long time. "I've never felt this way before, never expected to find someone like you."

"I'm far from perfect. You know my history." His eyes went somber.

"We're all far from perfect. And as long as you'll be open with me, we can face things together." She angled closer, sealing her mouth to his, holding, relishing the privacy but wishing they had more.

And they would, a prospect that filled her with passion and promise.

Easing back, Marshall stroked her hair from her face with reverent hands. "Move in with me. Help me build the family ranch back to the place full of life it used to be."

She sank into his arms, and into their future. "I can't think of anything that would bring me more joy."

Epilogue

Marshall couldn't remember a better Christmas since he'd been a child, and it was all thanks to Tally. Having her at his side—in his life—as he'd spent the day with his family had made the day complete.

And he couldn't think of a better way to finish off the holiday than lying together on the fur rug in front of the fireplace after making love. The peace in his heart and this amazing woman by his side were the best gifts of all. The future stretched ahead of him, and for the first time in too long, he allowed himself to live beyond the moment.

The tree they'd decorated together glowed with lights, the golden shimmer bathing her creamy body. He stroked along her spine, their legs tangled in the aftermath of their lovemaking. He fluffed the pillow under her head, making her smile.

Seeing her happy only multiplied his own pleasure.

She tipped her face toward his, her hair teasing along his arm. "Today was magical. Thank you."

"It's the first of many." He could see himself beside her for the long haul. No more hugging the wall.

"I like the sound of that."

The day after the fund-raiser, they'd celebrated by moving her things into his room and begun making plans for the future. She'd told him of her plans to apply for the scholarship to return to college to become a counselor. He'd offered to help her, but she'd been insistent about making her own way. He hadn't argued. For now.

Nugget stretched and wandered over, making himself comfortable on the blanket between their feet.

Marshall combed his fingers through her silky red hair. "I have a gift for you."

Sighing, she leaned into his touch. "But you already gave me a Christmas gift when you brought all those presents to the hospital, and the beautiful statue today."

He'd given her a sculpted stone statue of a mythical sea nymph in honor of her mermaid charm. The pleasure on her face, the gentle way she'd caressed it, had made it well worth the search.

Bringing her joy brought him joy.

"I wanted to save this for when we were alone."

He lifted his hat off the chair where he'd placed it to cover the small box, a piece of his past he wanted to share with her. Only her. He passed over the necklace box. "It was my mother's."

"Oh, Marshall…" Her voice quivered as her hand went to her mouth. "Are you sure you want to give this to me? Is your family okay with it?"

"Absolutely. I got it from my father today with his blessing." He creaked the box open to reveal a delicate platinum chain with a diamond heart.

"It's beautiful." She looked at him with tear-filled eyes. "Are you sure you want to—"

He stopped her. "Yes, I'm sure I want you to have it, and I'm certain my mother would, too."

"Thank you." She cradled his face in her hand. "I'm honored to wear it."

He pulled the chain from the box, unhooked the clasp, and placed the necklace on her, the heart nestling at the base of her neck. He could feel his mother smiling on this moment. She would have liked Tally and her gentle, take-charge way. She had already signed up for an Al-Anon group. She'd said she wanted to support him in every way possible. He didn't know what he'd done to be lucky enough to have her in his life, but he wasn't letting her go again.

She trailed her fingers down his arm, along where his cast had been removed just before Christmas Eve. "Now that you're healed, will you take me riding tomorrow?"

He didn't see the need to tell her he'd been riding with the cast on. "I would like that, very much."

"And I like the way you look in that cowboy hat of yours."

"Ah, so the ride is to fulfill a fantasy?" He dropped his Stetson on her head.

"You could say that," she answered playfully, wriggling closer.

An invitation he fully intended to accept.

He looked forward to a lifetime of making all her dreams come true.

* * * * *

*Passion and turmoil abound in the lives of the
Alaskan Oil Barons!
Nothing is as it seems.
Will they confront Milla Jones?
Is Uncle Lyle involved?
Why has Breanna stayed away from her family?
Find out the answers and so much more
in the final two stories
starring the Steeles and Mikkelsons!*

The Billionaire Renegade
(available January 2019)

The Secret Twin
(available February 2019)

*And don't miss a single twist in the
first six books of the Alaskan Oil Barons from*
USA TODAY *bestselling author Catherine Mann.*

The Baby Claim
The Double Deal
The Love Child
The Twin Birthright
The Second Chance
The Rancher's Seduction

ALASKAN OIL BARONS - STEELE MIKKELSON FAMILY TREE

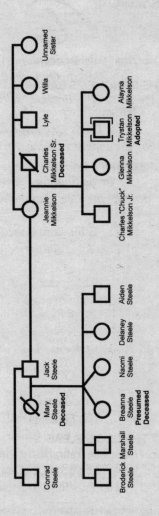

Get 4 FREE REWARDS!

We'll send you 2 FREE Books plus 2 FREE Mystery Gifts.

Harlequin® Desire books feature heroes who have it all: wealth, status, incredible good looks... everything but the right woman.

FREE
Value Over
$20

YES! Please send me 2 FREE Harlequin® Desire novels and my 2 FREE gifts (gifts are worth about $10 retail). After receiving them, if I don't wish to receive any more books, I can return the shipping statement marked "cancel." If I don't cancel, I will receive 6 brand-new novels every month and be billed just $4.55 per book in the U.S. or $5.24 per book in Canada. That's a savings of at least 13% off the cover price! It's quite a bargain! Shipping and handling is just 50¢ per book in the U.S. and 75¢ per book in Canada.* I understand that accepting the 2 free books and gifts places me under no obligation to buy anything. I can always return a shipment and cancel at any time. The free books and gifts are mine to keep no matter what I decide.

225/326 HDN GMYU

Name (please print)

Address   Apt. #

City   State/Province   Zip/Postal Code

Mail to the **Reader Service:**
IN U.S.A.: P.O. Box 1341, Buffalo, NY 14240-8531
IN CANADA: P.O. Box 603, Fort Erie, Ontario L2A 5X3

Want to try 2 free books from another series? Call 1-800-873-8635 or visit www.ReaderService.com.

---

*Terms and prices subject to change without notice. Prices do not include sales taxes, which will be charged (if applicable) based on your state or country of residence. Canadian residents will be charged applicable taxes. Offer not valid in Quebec. This offer is limited to one order per household. Books received may not be as shown. Not valid for current subscribers to Harlequin Desire books. All orders subject to approval. Credit or debit balances in a customer's account(s) may be offset by any other outstanding balance owed by or to the customer. Please allow 4 to 6 weeks for delivery. Offer available while quantities last.

Your Privacy—The Reader Service is committed to protecting your privacy. Our Privacy Policy is available online at www.ReaderService.com or upon request from the Reader Service. We make a portion of our mailing list available to reputable third parties that offer products we believe may interest you. If you prefer that we not exchange your name with third parties, or if you wish to clarify or modify your communication preferences, please visit us at www.ReaderService.com/consumerschoice or write to us at Reader Service Preference Service, P.O. Box 9062, Buffalo, NY 14240-9062. Include your complete name and address.

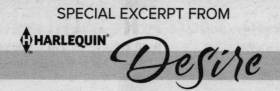
He would never forget the day, ten years ago, when Maya
Richardson had walked through his door looking for a
job. She'd been a godsend, helping Ayden grow Stewart
Investments into the company it was today. Thinking
of her brought a smile to Ayden's face. How could it
not? Not only was she the best assistant he'd ever had,
Maya had fascinated him. Utterly and completely. Maya
had hidden an exceptional figure beneath professional
clothing and kept her hair in a tight bun. But Ayden had
often wondered what it would be like to throw her over
his desk and muss her up. Five years ago, he hadn't gone
quite that far, but he had crossed a boundary.

Maya had been devastated over her breakup with her
boyfriend. She'd come to him for comfort, and, instead,
Ayden had made love to her. Years of wondering what
it would be like to be with Maya had erupted into a

passionate encounter. Their one night together had been so explosive that the next morning Ayden had needed to take a step back to regain his perspective. He'd had to put up his guard; otherwise, he would have hurt her badly. He thought he'd been doing the right thing, but Maya hadn't thought so. In retrospect, Ayden wished he'd never given in to temptation. But he had, and he'd lost a damn good assistant. Maya had quit, and Ayden hadn't seen or heard from her since.

Shaking his head, Ayden strode to his desk and picked up the phone, dialing the recruiter who'd helped him find Carolyn. He wasn't looking forward to this process. It had taken a long time to find and train Carolyn. Before her, Ayden had dealt with several candidates walking into his office thinking they could ensnare him.

No, he had someone else in mind. A hardworking, dedicated professional who could read his mind without him saying a word and who knew how to handle a situation in his absence. Someone who knew about the big client he'd always wanted to capture but never could attain. She also had a penchant for numbers and research like no one he'd ever seen, not even Carolyn.

Ayden knew exactly who he wanted. He just needed to find out where she'd escaped to.

Don't miss what happens next!
At the CEO's Pleasure *by Yahrah St. John,*
part of her Stewart Heirs series!

Available January 2019 wherever
Harlequin® Desire books and ebooks are sold.

www.Harlequin.com

Love Harlequin romance?

DISCOVER.

Be the first to find out about promotions, news and exclusive content!

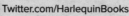 Facebook.com/HarlequinBooks

Twitter.com/HarlequinBooks

 Instagram.com/HarlequinBooks

Pinterest.com/HarlequinBooks

ReaderService.com

EXPLORE.

Sign up for the Harlequin e-newsletter and download a free book from any series at **TryHarlequin.com.**

CONNECT.

Join our Harlequin community to share your thoughts and connect with other romance readers!
Facebook.com/groups/HarlequinConnection

 **HARLEQUIN**®

**ROMANCE WHEN
YOU NEED IT**